DEDALUS EUR[...]

Sparrow

Robertson
EUROPEAN CLASSICS

Giovanni Verga

Sparrow
(*The Story of a Songbird*)

Translated from the Italian by
Christine Donougher

With an introduction by
Roderick Conway Morris

Dedalus / Hippocrene

Funded by THE ARTS COUNCIL OF ENGLAND

Published in the UK by Dedalus Limited, Langford Lodge, St Judith's Lane, Sawtry, Cambs, PE17 5XE

UK ISBN 1 873982 46 1

Published in the USA by Hippocrene Books Inc, 171 Madison Avenue, New York, NY 10016

US ISBN 0 7818 0295 4

Distributed in Canada by Marginal Distribution, Unit 103, 227 George Street North, Peterborough, Ontario, KJ9 3G9
Distributed in Australia & New Zealand by Peribo Pty Ltd, 26 Tepko Road, Terrey Hills, N.S.W. 2084

First published in Italy in 1871 as *La Storia di una Capinera*
First Dedalus edition in 1994

Translation copyright © Christine Donougher 1994
Introduction copyright © Dedalus 1994

Printed in Finland by Wsoy
Typeset by Datix International Limited, Bungay, Suffolk

This book is sold subject to the condition that it shall not, by way of trade or otherwise, be lent, resold, hired out, or otherwise circulated without the publisher's prior consent in any form of binding or cover other than that in which it is published and without a similar condition including this condition being imposed on the subsequent purchaser.

A C.I.P. listing for this title is available on request.

THE TRANSLATOR

Christine Donougher was born in England in 1954. She read English and French at Cambridge and after a career in publishing is now a freelance translator and editor.

Her many translations from French and Italian include the Sylvie Germain novels: *The Book of Nights* and *Days of Anger*; Jan Potocki's *Tales from the Saragossa Manuscript*, Octave Mirbeau's *Le Calvaire* and Camillo Boito's *Senso* (*and other stories*).

Her current projects include editing *The Dedalus Book of French Fantasy* and translating Sylvie Germain's *Nuit d'ambre*.

THE EDITOR

Roderick Conway Morris lives in Venice and writes about Italian art and culture for *The International Herald Tribune*, *The New York Times* and *The Spectator*.

He is the author of the novel *Jem: Memoirs of an Ottoman Secret Agent*.

Contents

INTRODUCTION

by Roderick Conway Morris

I

When *Storia di una Capinera* came out in book form in 1871 (having been run in instalments in a magazines the year before), it was Giovanni Verga's fourth published novel, but the first for which he received any money – 100 lire from the Milan publisher A. Lumpugnani. Verga was then 31, having written his first (unpublished) novel at the age of sixteen. The new work was a landmark not merely in financial terms – it heralded the beginning of his most artistically fruitful period, which was to last until the early 1890s, during which time he was to write *I Malavoglia*, *Maestro-don Gesualdo* and *Cavalleria Rustica*, and establish himself as one of Italy's foremost writers, a reputation he enjoys to this day.

Storia di una Capinera – the tale of a child put into a convent after the death of her mother, and destined to become a nun, whether she wishes to or not, on account of the cruelty of her stepmother, who is solely interested in her own son and daughter, and the weakness of her father, who has married a second wife socially and economically his superior, and to whom he defers in everything – is, then, the work of a writer on the point of emerging from the chrysalis of his formative years to reveal the full measure of his genius.

Or as Franco Zeffirelli put it, shortly after he had finished *Sparrow*, his film of the story (a project that he had been planning for many years): 'This is the portrait of a girl, the portrait of a summer, the only summer of happiness in her life. It's not one of the Verga grand family sagas that came soon after – it's an exquisite watercolour, the tragedy of a little girl . . . And yet a story rich in feeling and drama.'

II

At first glance the novel might seem the kind of sentimental tear-jerker that was popular at the time – and so it would have been if its theme had been attempted by a less gifted writer. It is, in fact, a more subtle and accomplished work than meets the eye, and its successful completion not only brought Verga public recognition, but confirmed his own faith in the potential of his talents.

Sentimentality thrives on vagueness, the soft focus – but the perception here of people, the countryside, the grim realities of convent life, are surprisingly sharp, and the cumulative effect infinitely more memorable and disturbing than the average, formulaic weepy. Nor should we be fooled by the gushing naivety of the girl's first-person narrative – a style adopted to convince the reader that these really are the letters of a pathetically ingenuous young person – which artfully conveys the solitary blossoming of a human being, whilst slowly but surely building a picture of a world outside of appalling indifference, blind and deaf to her unmerited suffering.

Yet, the chief impact of the novel derives from the inescapable fact that, however extravagant and emotionally overcharged the text might sometimes seem, it is firmly based in a cruel social reality, and is giving a voice to generations of immured girls and women whose tribulations have otherwise scarcely been recorded.

It had long been the custom in Catholic Europe for superfluous offspring to become priests, monks and nuns, regardless of whether they showed any real evidence of a vocation, but even as this tradition began to decline in much of the rest of Italy, in Sicily it persisted. In aristocratic families the eldest son was expected to inherit everything, while his siblings (especially girls who could not be provided with dowries) frequently sank into the position of unwanted poor relations, who could only expect the most meagre provision, and were commonly directed, even forcibly, to religious institutions, where their daily sustenance, however modest, was guaranteed. As is the way of the world, this practice was imitated by the bourgeoisie (of the kind depicted in Verga's novel), even though they did not have quite the same horror of marrying beneath them that haunted the declining and increasingly impoverished nobility.

The convents of Sicily had become, as a result, human dustbins, Mediterranean Dothegirls Halls, ever ready to receive the island's 'excess' female population. The position was ameliorated by national legislation in 1867, which curbed the activities of such institutions – just a couple of years before Verga sat down to write his story. Yet, not only did convents offer stubborn resistance to the reforms, and obtain the right to continue more or less as they were until the last existing sisters died, but they also, especially in the south, went on receiving girls pressed into taking the veil. (Thus, it was an extremely optimistic or disingenuous reviewer who, on the publication of *Storia di una Capinera*, dared claim that the problem had already 'ceased to exist'.)

Verga's mother, Donna Caterina, like her father a descendant of the minor nobility, had been educated by nuns. Two of his aunts had taken the veil, one in Vizzini, the other in Palermo, and a third, after time in a convent, remained, unmarried, with the Vergas. The convent in which his mother had been raised was directly opposite the family house in Catania. The family attended mass there, hearing the singing of the postulants and nuns, hidden from view behind the grilles. This sequestered community permanently on the Verga doorstep clearly aroused the young writer's curiosity, an interest increased by his mother's accounts of her life there. Donna Caterina was a devout woman, but an avid reader and an 'intellectual' by the standards of her time and place – she had, for example, as a family friend Emilio del Cerro recorded, made sure to obtain a copy of Ernesto Renan's *Life of Jesus* when it was causing outrage and being declared sacrilegious in Catania ('especially among those who had not read it'), in order to judge for herself.

And, as Federico De Roberto, Verga's younger friend and author of *I Viceré*, recalled in an article, on the genesis of *Storia di una Capinera*, written in 1922 (the year of Verga's death): 'A sincere believer, Donna Caterina did not, however, conceal her condemnation of certain harsh aspects of convent education. The little girls were deprived of embraces and kisses in accordance with the regulations; of the world seen only through grilles they knew nothing beyond the terror of mortal sins; they saw nothing beyond some roofs and terraces visible from the belvedere. Only those who had to spend the rest of their lives there inside, the Chosen, had any privileges: but far too many "vocations" were not spontaneous, indeed were prompted by devious stratagems, with sometimes appalling results: wasting sicknesses and madness. Among the cells was one that the girls never went near willingly, because it bore a terrible name: "the madwoman's cell", and it was never empty. From within it you could hear blood-curdling shrieks, feeble moans and ghastly bursts of laughter.'

Once he embarked on the novel, Verga did not rely on memory alone of what his mother had told him, but made considerable efforts to check details in the interests of authenticity, writing to Donna Caterina from Florence in June 1869, to take but one example, to ask 'whether it is the custom in Catania to go and inform close relatives living in a convent of a forthcoming family wedding; and if on this formal visit the groom would go too, when the relatives inside were the bride's, or only the bride, or only her family . . .'

Verga also drew important inspiration for the novel from key experiences that matured in his mind after he first left Sicily to seek his fortune as a writer on the mainland. In 1854, 1855 and 1867 the Verga family moved out of the sea-port of Catania: on the first two occasions to their country property in the hills at Vizzini, south-west of Catania, and on the last to Trecastagne, on the slopes of Mount Etna (this dramatic landscape was to form the setting of the novel), to escape cholera outbreaks in the city, when, as described in the book, the authorities also ordered colleges and convents to open their doors and send their charges to places free from contagion.

During one of these extended rustic sojourns, Verga, then just fifteen, appears to have encountered the daughter of a neighbouring family, still in her convent dress, pale-skinned, dark-haired and beautiful. Adoring her from afar during the several months of their stay, he finally came to put his arm round her waist at a dance, an indescribably exciting, almost mystical moment for him. When the epidemic subsided the girl duly returned to her convent, eventually to become a nun – Verga later catching, however, fleeting glimpses of her in the parlour while visiting his aunt Donna Rosalia Verga, who had taken the name Sister Carmela, and happened to be in the same convent.

The truth and detail of these brief encounters with an unattainable, forbidden amour are difficult to assess, and very likely became heightened in the writer's memory. But whether Verga was drawing on actual events or not, the evocation of the confused agony of dawning adolescent sexuality, which in his imagined heroine (doomed to a life sentence of chastity) takes on a febrile, almost gothic intensity, constitutes one of the most daring and striking elements of the book.

III

This fourth novel also marks a turning point in Verga's career in another respect, for with it, after experimenting with a love story in his previous novel *Una Peccatrice*, he definitively left behind the political novels of his youth.

Verga was born into an Italy most of which had long been under foreign domination – by this period, that of the Austrians in the north and the Bourbons in the south. Both were oppressive regimes, Bourbon rule being nicely described by a local journalist as 'the negation of God erected into a system of government' (a phrase that caught the eye of Gladstone, who was in Naples to witness the trial of dissidents, and which is often erroneously attributed to him).

Growing patriotic fervour culminated in the revolutionary uprisings that took place all over Italy, coinciding with similar outbreaks in other parts of Europe, in 1848–9. As elsewhere, the Italian risings were duly quelled – and only in the Piedmont were the Austrians forced to cede territory. It was against this background that in 1857 Verga wrote his first, unpublished, juvenile novel, *Amore e Patria*, a celebration of the American War of Independence, of little literary value, but passionately imbued with the nationalist aspirations of the times.

Two years later Piedmont, under the constitutional monarch Victor Emmanuel II, began to re-arm, notably with the creation of an Alpine corps under the command of the nationalist hero, Giuseppe Garibaldi. Austria attacked, initiating a war in which the Italians, with the support of the French, made considerable gains. In exchange for ceding Nice and Savoy to France in a post-war settlement, Victor Emmanuel was left with the enlarged Kingdom of Sardinia comprising six regions: Emilia-Romagna, Liguria, Lombardy, Piedmont, Sardinia and Tuscany.

These successes in the north inspired insurrection in Sicily, which Garibaldi was despatched to support. In May 1860, he landed in Marsala with his celebrated One Thousand, and despite being vastly outnumbered by Bourbon forces succeeded in taking Palermo, then returning to the mainland to continue his war of liberation, entering Naples in triumph on 7 September.

When the Bourbons withdrew from Catania, Verga, then aged twenty, was among those who enlisted to join the National Guard, with the task of maintaining public order, in which he continued to serve for some four years. As a journalist, too, he supported the nationalist cause: in 1860 he was co-founder and co-editor of a weekly political magazine, *Roma degli Italiani* – with which his association ended after only a few months because of differences of

14

opinion with the magazine's financial backers, who were republican Sicilian nationalists, critical of the annexation of Sicily to the Kingdom of Italy. Two other publishing ventures that he embarked on were similarly short-lived.

In the meantime he continued to write novels: *I Carbonari della Montagana*, which appeared in 1862, published in Catania at his own expense, and *Sulle Lagune*, issued in instalments from January to March 1863, both patriotic in inspiration. By the time his fourth novel, *Una Peccatrice*, was published in 1866, Verga had begun to travel outside Sicily, to Florence, the new capital of Italy (transferred from Turin), though still returning regularly to Catania. Florence became during this period the country's cultural capital, and a magnet for aspiring young writers and artists, Verga's mother tongue was Sicilian dialect, and he also hoped to improve his Italian by immersing himself in the heart of Tuscany − Tuscan dialect being, since the time of Dante, Petrarch and Boccaccio the basis of Italian, the peninsula's modern lingua franca. In this he was successful − though he still cherished an affection for Sicilian, and in his writing as well as in his speech he maintained certain mannerisms of his native language.

IV

One of his most important introductions in Florence was to Francesco Dall'Ongaro, a writer who has since fallen into comparative obscurity but who was then much admired not only for his literary achievements but also as a journalist, nationalist activist and friend of the common people. A reforming priest who found himself at odds with the Church hierarchy and abandoned his ministry, Dall'Ongaro nevertheless continued to preach moral virtue and patriotic values. Of Friulian origin, he was for many years, in Trieste, editor of a periodical, *La Favilla*, to which Caterina Percoto, another Friulian writer, of aristocratic background, became a regular contributor. Dall'Ongaro advised her to write about the countryside and the country people around her, and this indeed became the material of her short stories. Educated by nuns, at the convent of Santa Chiara in Udine, Caterina Percoto never married, choosing instead to retire to the countryside to look after her ailing mother, and dedicating herself to writing a great many short stories, some in Italian and some in Friulian dialect.

Dall'Ongaro greatly encouraged Verga in his literary endeavours, assisting him most notably with the publication of *Storia di una Capinera*, and providing a preface for the bound edition, in the guise of a letter addressed to Caterina Percoto, whose reply was also included.

V

The novel was an instant commercial and critical success, receiving fulsome praise in papers and periodicals all over Italy, with only one or two dissenting voices making themselves heard. Almost to a man and woman, the literary critics fell under its spell. Vittorio Bersezio, in the *Gazetta Piemontese* spoke for many of his colleagues when he wrote that he had not for a very long time read a book 'with such emotion'; Raffaelo Barbiera in the *Scena* in Venice called it 'beautiful for the genuineness of its passion, affecting simplicity and purity of language'; and an anonymous reviewer 'A.W.' in the *Revista Europa* (which had serialized *Sulle Lagune*) declared the book 'written with grace, delicately felt, describing in a true, natural and most effective way, the torment of the cloister.' One critic was so moved as to express his plaudits in verse. And even an otherwise curmudgeonly commentator, Angelo de Gubernatis, reviewing Italy's literary output in 1872 for *The Athenaeum* in London, whilst expressing his general distaste for modern Italian novels, which he thought all alike in the carelessness of their structure, weakness of plot and total absence of good taste, made two exceptions: del Barrilli's *Val d'Olivi* and Verga's *Capinera*, which he found no less original than

16

it was poetical, and head and shoulders above what de Gubernatis saw as the generally vulgar and fatuous efforts of other Italian prose writers.

The lavish encomiums did not give Verga, always very self-critical, an inflated opinion of himself, and in a letter of 1872 to his close friend the writer Luigi Capuana (born in Catania the year before Verga), he attributed the book's warm reception to the subject matter rather than his own talents: 'I am beginning to understand why this poor little book of mine has been fortunate, attracting to itself all the merit of its theme, which, especially for us in Sicily is of considerable interest.' And again, in the following year, he wrote to Emilio Treves, who was to publish the classic novels destined to win Verga lasting fame, that whatever faults the critics could find in his works to date, 'I can find quite a few more than they can, and am trying to do better.'

Bibliographical Note

The most readily available Italian edition of *Storia di una Capinera* is at present published in paperback in Arnoldo Mondadori's Oscar Classici series (Milan, 1991). Introduced by Sergio Pautasso, the book contains a useful bibliography of Verga's works, biographers and critical commentators.

Epistolary preface to the first edition of *Storia di una Capinera*, written by Francesco Dall'Ongaro and addressed to Caterina Percoto.

My dearest friend,
A year ago, a young Sicilian, of gentle manner and demeanour, entrusted me with some pages, asking me to read through them, and to offer an opinion on the sad story they contained.

They were the letters of a young Sicilian nun, written to a friend and companion. I thought at first of sending those pages, telling of a life of sorrow and abnegation, to you with your knowledge of this subject. But then I was so moved by the letters, or rather by the facts they vividly describe, that I couldn't put them down until I'd read them all, the last one causing even an experienced writer like me to shed genuine tears.

This was how I expressed my opinion: instead of sending you the manuscript as it was, I gave it to our friend Lampunani to print, and in order that he might give the widest circulation to the emotion that had overwhelmed my own heart at that first reading.

Now you can read the letters, published in this handsome volume that you might wish to preface with your good wishes to the author, who joins forces with us.

Francesco Dall'Ongaro

Rome, 25 November, 1871

Caterina Percoto's response and verdict, dated 2 March 1872:

Dear Sir,
Your lovely Sparrow owes her success to the skill of your pen, which makes me feel I'm in Sicily, and deals so compassionately with one of the worst afflictions suffered by those of my sex in our society. Here, in the Veneto, thanks to the Code Napoleon, the dismal practice of sacrificing our poor young girls to monastic life has ceased for some time now, but the barbaric custom of raising women for enclosed orders still continues.

You, who are young and blessed with a gift for words so engaging, so true, so effective, will be our champion. Italy will be grateful to you, and Dall'Ongaro and I will be very happy to have been among the first to recognize you as one of our most talented writers.

Caterina Percoto

I had seen a poor songbird locked in a cage: it was fearful, sad, ailing, with a look of terror in its eye. It cowered in a corner of its cage, and when it heard the cheerful song of the other little birds twittering in the green meadow or the azure sky, it watched them with what seemed a tearful gaze. But it dared not rebel, it dared not break the wire that held it captive, poor creature. Yet its captors loved it – they were sweet children, who toyed with its sorrow, and recompensed it for its melancholy with breadcrumbs and kind words. The poor songbird tried to resign itself. It was not ill-natured, it did not even mean to reproach them with its sorrow, for it tried to peck sadly at the odd seed or breadcrumb; it could not swallow them. After two days it tucked its head under its wing and the next day it was found stone-dead in its prison.

The poor songbird had died! Yet its bowl was full. It had died because within that tiny body was something that needed not only grain to live on, and that suffered from something other than hunger and thirst.

The mother of those two children that had been the poor little bird's innocent but merciless executioners told me the story of an unhappy girl whose body had been imprisoned within the walls of a convent, and whose spirit had been tortured by superstition and love – one of those intimate stories that pass unnoticed every day – the story of a shy and tender heart, of one who had loved and wept and prayed, without daring to let her tears be seen or her prayers heard, who had eventually withdrawn into her sorrow and died. And I thought then of the poor songbird that would gaze at the sky through the bars of its prison, that would not sing, that would peck sadly at its grain, that had tucked its head under its wing and died.

That is why I have called it *Storia di una Capinera* – The Story of a Songbird.

My dear Marianna,

I promised to write to you, and, you see, I'm keeping my promise! In the three weeks I've spent here, running about the countryside – alone! all alone, mind you! – from dawn till dusk, sitting on the grass beneath these huge chestnut trees, listening to the birds singing with happiness, as they hop about, like me, giving thanks to the good Lord, I haven't found a moment, not a single moment, to tell you that I love you a hundred times more, now that I'm far away from you, and don't have you beside me every hour of the day, as I used to, there, in the convent. How happy I should be if you were here with me, gathering wild flowers, chasing butterflies, daydreaming in the shade of these trees when the sun beats down, and strolling arm in arm on these lovely evenings, by moonlight, with no other sound but the droning of insects – a melodious sound to me, because it means that I'm in the countryside, out in the open air – and the song of that melancholy bird I don't know the name of, but which brings the sweetest tears to my eyes when I stand at my window at night, listening to it. How beautiful the countryside is, Marianna! If only you were here with me! If only you could see these mountains, in the moonshine or at sunrise, and the ample shade of the woods, and the azure-blue of the sky, and the green of the vines hidden in the valleys, all around the little houses, and the deep-blue of the sea glistening over there, far away in the distance, and all these villages climbing up the sides of the mountains – big mountains that seem tiny beside our majestic old Etna! If only you could see how beautiful our Mount Etna is at close quarters! From the belvedere at the convent, it appeared to be a huge, isolated peak, always snow-capped. Now I can count the tops of all the little mountains around it. I can see its deep valleys and wooded slopes, its proud summit on which the snow, reaching down into the gullies, marks out great brown patches.

Everything here is beautiful – the air, the light, the sky, the trees, mountains and valleys, and the sea! When I thank the Lord for all these beautiful things, I do so with a word, a tear, a look, alone in the middle of the countryside, kneeling on the moss in the woods, or sitting on the grass. I think that the good Lord must be more pleased, because I thank him with my whole heart, and my thoughts are not imprisoned beneath the dark vault of the chancel, but reach up into the lofty shade of these trees, and out into all the vastness of this sky and these horizons. They call us God's chosen, because we're destined to be wedded to the Lord, but did not the good Lord create all these beautiful things for everybody? And why should his brides be deprived of them?

Oh goodness! How happy I am! Do you remember Rosalia, who tried to convince us that the world outside the convent had greater charms? We couldn't imagine it, do you recall? And we laughed at her! If I hadn't been out of the convent, I'd never have believed it possible that Rosalia was right. Our world was so restricted: the little altar, those poor flowers, deprived of fresh air, languishing in their vases, the belvedere from which we could see a mass of rooftops, and then away in the distance, as though in a magic lantern, the countryside, the sea, and all the beautiful things that God created. And there was our little garden, a hundred paces from end to end, and purposely arranged, it seemed, so that the walls of the convent could be seen above the trees, where we were allowed to stroll for an hour under the supervision of the Novice Mistress, but without being able to run about and enjoy ourselves. And that was all!

And, you know . . . I'm not sure that we were right not to give a little more thought to our families. It's true, I've had the greatest misfortune of all the postulants, because I lost my mother. But I feel now that I love my papa much more than I love Mother Superior, my sisters and my confessor. I feel that I love my dear papa with more trust and greater fondness, even though I can't claim to have had close contact with him for more than three weeks. You know that I was put inside the convent before I had even turned seven, when I was left on my own by my poor mama. They said they were giving me another family, and other mamas who would love me ... Yes, that's true ... But the love I feel for my father makes me realize how very different my poor mother's affection would have been.

You can't imagine the feeling inside me when my dear papa wishes me good morning and gives me a hug. As you know, Marianna, no one there ever used to hug us. It's against the rule ... Yet I can't see what's wrong with feeling so loved.

My stepmother is an excellent woman, because she's only concerned about Giuditta and Gigi, and lets me run about the vineyards as I please. My God! If she forbade me, as she forbids her children, to go skipping across the fields, in case they should fall, or catch sunstroke — I'd be very unhappy, wouldn't I? But she's probably kinder and more lenient with me because she knows that I won't be able to enjoy these pleasures for long, and that I'll be going back to being shut up inside again ...

But don't let's think of such horrible things. Now I'm cheerful and happy, and I'm amazed at how everyone's afraid of the cholera and curses it ... Thank goodness for the cholera that brought me here, into the countryside! If only it would go on all year!

No, that's wrong! Forgive me, Marianna. Who knows how many poor people are in tears while I laugh and have fun? My God! I must be really perverse if I can't be happy except when everyone else is suffering. Don't tell me that I'm wicked. I only want to be like everyone else, nothing more, and to enjoy these blessings that the Lord has given to us all — fresh air, light, freedom!

See how sad my letter's become, without my noticing. Don't pay any attention, Marianna. Skip right over that bit, which I shall put a big cross through, like so ... Now, to make up for that, I'll show you round our lovely little house.

You've never been to Monte Ilice, poor thing! What ever were your parents thinking of, taking you off to Mascalucia? A village, with houses backing on to other houses, streets, and churches – we've seen far too much of that! You should have come here, to the country, in the mountains, where to get to the nearest house you have to run through vineyards, jump across ditches, climb over walls, where there's no sound of carriages, or of bells ringing, nor voices of strangers, of any outsiders. Such is the countryside! We live in a pretty little house on the hillside, among vineyards, on the edge of the chestnut grove. It's a tiny little house, but so airy, and bright, and gay. From every door and window you can see the country-side, mountains, trees, and sky, and not just walls, those grim, blackened walls! In front there's a little lawn and a group of chestnut trees that cover the roof with an umbrella of branches and leaves, in which little birds twitter all the blessed day, without ever tiring. I have a sweet little room, that my bed only just fits into, with a wonderful window looking out over the chestnut grove. My sister Giuditta sleeps in a lovely big room next to mine, but I wouldn't swop my little box, as papa jokingly calls it, for that lovely room of hers. Anyway, she needs plenty of space for all her dresses and hats, while I have only to fold my tunic on a stool at the foot of my bed, and I'm done. But at night, when I listen at the window to all those leaves rustling, and amid the shadows that take on fantastic shapes I glimpse a moonbeam slipping through the branches like a white ghost, and when I listen to that nightingale trilling away in the distance, my head is filled with such imaginings, with such dreams and enchantments, that if I weren't afraid, I'd gladly stay at the window until daybreak.

On the far side of the lawn there's a pretty cottage with a roof of straw and rushes, where the steward's little family lives. If only you could see it – you'd see how tiny it is, and yet so clean, and how neat and tidy everything is there! The baby's cradle, the straw mattress, the work-table! I'd swop my little room for that cottage. I think that family, living together on those few square feet of land, must love each other all the more and be much happier; that in that limited space all their feelings must be deeper, and more absolute; that to a heart overwhelmed and almost bewildered by the daily spectacle of that vast horizon, it must be a joy and a comfort to withdraw into itself, to take refuge in its affections, within the confines of a small space, among the few objects that form the most intimate part of its identity, and that it must feel more complete in being near to them.

What is all this? What ever am I writing, Marianna? You'll be laughing at me and calling me a female Saint Augustine. My dear friend, forgive me. My heart's so full that I succumb, without realizing it, to the need to impart to you all the new emotions that I'm experiencing. During the first few days after I left the convent and came here, I was overawed, dazed, in a dream, as though transplanted to another world. I was disturbed and confused by everything. Imagine someone born blind, and who by a miracle starts to see! Now I've grown familiar with all these new impressions. Now my heart feels lighter, and my soul purer. I talk to myself, and I examine my conscience – not the timid, fearful way we used to in the convent, full of repentance and remorse; I examine it with contentment and happiness, praising the Lord for these blessings, and with the sense of being raised up to Him by the shedding of a tear, or by simply gazing at the moon and the starry firmament.

My God! Could this joyfulness be a sin? Could the Lord possibly be offended to see that rather than the convent, rather than silence, solitude and contemplation, I prefer the countryside, fresh air, and my family! If our kind-hearted old confessor were here, perhaps he could resolve my perplexity and dispel my confusion, perhaps he could advise and comfort me ... Whenever these doubts assail me, whenever I'm tormented by these uncertainties, I pray to the Lord for His enlightenment, help and guidance. Will you also pray for me, Marianna.

Meanwhile, I give Him praise and thanks and glory, I entreat Him to let me die here, or, if I must take my solemn vows and renounce these blessings for ever, to give me the strength and willingness and resignation to shut myself away in the convent and dedicate myself utterly to Him alone. I'll not be worthy of such grace; I'll be a sinner . . . but when, at nightfall, I see the steward's wife reciting the rosary, seated by the hearth on which her husband's soup is cooking, with her eldest boy on her lap and her baby asleep in the cradle that she rocks with her foot, I think the prayers of that woman – calm, serene and full of gratitude for the good Lord's bounty – must rise up to Him much purer than mine, which are full of misgivings, anxieties and yearnings that ill become me as a postulant, and that I can't completely defend myself against.

Look what a long letter I've written to you! Now, don't be cross with me any more, and send me back an even longer letter than mine. Tell me about yourself and your parents, your pleasures and your little troubles, as we used to every day in the convent, in recreation time, with our arms around each other. You see, I feel as though I've had a long chat with you, holding hands, just as before, and that you've been listening with that cheerful and mischievous little smile on your lips, as usual. So chat to me, send a good four pages (I shan't settle for any less, mind!) telling me everything you would have said to me. Give me all your news. Tell me what you see, what you think, how you spend the time, whether you're bored, or enjoying yourself, whether you're contented, and as happy as I am – whether you ever think of your friend Maria. Tell me the colour of your dress, because I know that you have one, now that you're a real young lady! Tell me whether you have lovely flowers in your garden, whether Mascalucia has chestnut trees, as we do here, and whether you took part in the grape harvest. You talk, and I'll listen. Don't keep me waiting on tenterhooks for too long.

Farewell, farewell, my dear Marianna, my beloved sister.

I send you a hundred kisses, on condition that you return
them.

Yours,

Maria

Dear Marianna,

The only news we're getting here is bad news, and all we see are frightened faces. The cholera is rampant in Catania. There's general terror and desolation.

Otherwise, were it not for these faces, and these fears, what more blessed life could there be than the one we live here? Papa goes hunting, or accompanies me on long walks when I might be afraid of getting lost in the woods. My little brother Gigi runs about, yelling and shouting, and climbs trees, and is always tearing his clothes, and mama ... (Marianna, if you only knew how difficult it is for me to call my stepmother by this sweet name! It's as though I'm wronging the memory of my poor mother ... And yet this is what I must call her!) ... mama scolds him, and gives him sweets and kisses and smacks, and mends his clothes and cleans them, umpteen times a day. She does nothing but sew and cosset her children – lucky things! And often while she's keeping an eye on the cooking, or on the maid who prepares the meal, she reproaches me for being useless, and not even able to cook ... Unfortunately, it's true. She's right. I do nothing but go running through the fields, picking wild flowers, and listening to the birds singing ... at my age! Do you know, I'm nearly twenty? It makes me feel ashamed of myself. But my dear papa doesn't have the heart to get cross with me – he can only kiss me and say, 'Poor child! Let her enjoy these few days of freedom!'

Tears come to my eyes whenever I think of my poor mama resting in the churchyard in Catania. But I think of her more often here, because I feel a stranger in my father's house. It's nobody's fault. They're not used to seeing me and having me under their feet – that's all. Anyway, if my stepmother tells me off for being useless, she has her reasons; it's for my own good, and after all I am at fault.

Not being a madcap like me, my sister's not very

effusive, but she loves me and doesn't complain about the inconvenience I cause her by occupying this small room where my trestle-bed has been squeezed in – before, she used it as a dressing-room, and now all her boxes and clothing are cluttering up her bedroom.

Gigi is still the sweet little boy that you knew, as happy and boisterous as ever. He flings his arms round my neck twenty times a day, and consoles me with a kiss when his mother shouts at me on account of his torn clothes. But is it my fault I wasn't taught at the convent how to mend things? It really should be my job. Giuditta's a young lady, and anyway she's far too busy all day long with her wardrobe and arranging her hair, and she's right to spend so much time on them because pretty dresses and ribbons suit her so well, you'd think they were meant for her . . . And besides, she has a rich dowry from her mother – as you know, my papa is only a very humble clerk. So what else should she be thinking of at her age? While she was trying on a new dress, the day before yesterday, she looked so beautiful that I asked if I could kiss her! She quite rightly said no, so as not to get the material creased. What a silly goose I am, Marianna! As though her dress were like my dowdy twill tunic that's never in any danger of creasing!

Oh, what a blessing it is to have a family! In the evening, when papa locks the door, I feel an indescribable contentment, as though the ties binding me to my loved ones in the intimacy of home life were drawn tighter. Yet what a gloomy sense of sadness all we poor recluses used to feel – do you remember? – at the rattling of the porter's bunch of keys and the grating of the locks! Then with a wringing of my heart, my thoughts would fly to the poor wretches in prison. I've confessed to this a hundred times, and done a hundred penances for it, but I just can't help it. Here, in the morning, when I'm wakened by the twittering of the little birds fighting over the breadcrumbs I leave out for them on the windowsill, before I open my eyes my very first thought is of the happiness of being with my family, close to my father, my little brother, and Giuditta, who will kiss me and wish me good morning; knowing that I shan't have any offices to recite, or contemplation to do, or silences to observe, and that as soon as I've jumped out of bed, I'll open my window to let in that balmy air, that ray of sunshine, that rustling of leaves, and that birdsong; that I'll be able to go out alone, whenever I want, to run and skip wherever I please, and that I won't encounter any austere faces, or black robes, or dark corridors . . . Marianna, I've a terrible sin to confess to you! If only I could have a lovely coffee-coloured petticoat – not with a hoop, I don't mean that! – but a petticoat that wasn't black, in which I could run about and climb over walls, that didn't keep reminding me, as this ugly tunic does, that, once the cholera has passed, the convent awaits me back in Catania . . .

Let's not think about that! I'm a reckless madcap! Forgive me, my dear Marianna, I was only joking. But I haven't yet told you that I have a sweet little bird, a bright and lively pet sparrow that's very fond of me and answers to my call. He comes flying to take titbits from my hands, nibbles my fingers and playfully ruffles my hair. Actually, he has a rather sad story, to begin with: papa brought him to me wrapped in a handkerchief, and the handkerchief was stained with blood. It was probably the first time that the poor little thing had tried to fly, and a gun-shot had injured his wing. Fortunately, it wasn't a serious injury. What nasty, barbaric pastimes men have! At the sight of that blood, and the sound of that cheeping – the poor little thing must have been in great pain – I wept in sympathy, and I even began to blame my dear papa. Everyone was laughing at me, even Gigi. I bathed the wing, but I wasn't hopeful that the poor little thing would survive. Yet here he is, hopping about now, making a great racket! Sometimes he's still troubled by his injury, and comes and nestles in my lap, cheeping and dragging his wing, as though trying to share his pain with me. I comfort him with kisses, stroke him, and feed him breadcrumbs and grain, then he spryly goes off and settles on my windowsill, and turns to me, chirping, flapping his wings and stetching out his neck, with his mouth wide open.

The day before yesterday, a big ugly cat gave me a great scare. Carino (that's what I call my sparrow) was on the table, playfully mixing up all the cards – he's a great prankster! – getting them into a muddle, and twittering constantly. Then the little rascal would turn to look at me with his small, bright eyes, as though he enjoyed teasing me. All of a sudden, with a single bound, that big black cat was on the table, reaching out its paw to seize him. I screamed, and poor Carino screeched as well, and was very quick to take refuge with me. I don't know how I managed to hide him in my hands, under my apron, but we were both trembling. The whole household came running at my cry. My stepmother scolded me for having needlessly frightened her, and told me that I was too old for such childishness, and that if the cat had caught Carino, it would only have been doing as it ought to. Giuditta was laughing, and that naughty little boy, Gigi, kept urging the cat to snatch the little bird out of my lap. I could feel him in my hands quivering from the great fright he'd been given, and his heart was beating furiously. I'd sooner have died than surrender him! Ever since that day, I never forget to lock the door of my room, where I leave Carino. I hate that cat!

On the other hand, I really love the steward's dog, which is a great big farm-dog that's completely black, and stands so high. At first he really terrified me with his snarling, but now he's very affectionate towards me: he wags his tail and licks my hand, and rubs his sides against my tunic, telling me with those intelligent eyes of his that he loves me. In fact, he's my guardian. He accompanies me on my walks, and always stays close to me. He runs on ahead to explore the ground, then comes bounding back, wagging his tail and barking happily. When I call him, he knows that it's time for our walk (this happens twenty times a day), and you should see how he barks and jumps up and fawns on me!

I've told you all about my dog and my sparrow, about that horrible cat, and I still haven't mentioned that we have country neighbours who often come to visit, and that we spend almost every evening playing games together, and that we go for lovely walks at sunset. They live in a house not far from us, at the bottom of the valley – you can see it from my window. Their name is Valentini – do you know them? Papa and mama say they're very nice people. They have a daughter, Annetta, who's almost my age, and she and I are good friends. Not like you and me, though! You needn't be jealous, because I love you much more, and I want you to love me much more than all your other friends. When will you write back? Last time, you kept me waiting two whole weeks. See how quickly I reply, and what a long letter I've written. If you keep me waiting another fortnight to tell me that you return my love and the hundreds of kisses I send you, then I'll love my new friend more than you. So, be warned!

P.S. I forgot to tell you that, apart from Annetta, the Valentini also have a son, a young man who has often come with his sister, and whose name is Antonio, but they call him Nino.

Marianna, why aren't you here to come for walks, and have fun, and enjoy yourself with us? Why can't I hug you and say to you at every moment: Isn't this beautiful? Isn't that fun?... and let you see how happy I am — my goodness, as happy as anyone could ever wish to be. So imagine if you were here!

Yesterday as the sun was going down, we went for a lovely walk in the chestnut grove with the Valentini. How beautiful the grove is! If only you could have seen it, Marianna: a delicious shade, a few dying rays of sunlight filtering through the leaves, a perpetual, low-pitched sighing of the topmost branches, birds singing, and now and again a deep and solemn silence. You might almost feel afraid, beneath that huge vault of branches, among those endlessly crisscrossing paths, if even your fear weren't so pleasant. The dry leaves scrunched under our footsteps. Occasionally, some startled bird would take flight, shaking the few leaves that were hiding it and causing a sudden rustle. Our fine dog, Vigilante, ran blithely on ahead, barking after frightened blackbirds. Annetta, Gigi and Giuditta walked arm in arm, singing to themselves. Signor Nino followed them, with his rifle slung across his shoulder. The rest of the group were left far behind, and they kept shouting to us not to go so fast, because it was a tiring climb. Signor Nino also has a fine dog, a splendid gundog, with long ears and black spots all over. It's called Ali, and has already struck up a close friendship with Vigilante. At every step, Giuditta and Annetta in their long dresses would get caught in the undergrowth. Not me, though, I assure you! I run and skip, and never falter, and nor do the hedgerows leave any mark on my tunic. Signor Nino came up to me and told me to take care not to fall, he was afraid for me, poor fellow! If I hadn't been so embarrassed, I'd almost have challenged that young man to a race! Giuditta continually complained of feeling tired. What's wrong with these women, Marianna? They can't walk ten paces without the need of a man's arm, and without catching their clothes on every bramble! Thank goodness for my tunic! Signor Nino repeatedly offered me his arm – as if I had any need of it, indeed! I'm sure he was just trying to annoy me, otherwise why didn't he offer his arm to my sister, who was complaining about the climb – she was the one that needed it.

What a magnificent sight when we reached the top of the mountain! The chestnut grove doesn't extend all the way up, and from the summit you get an unimpeded view of the horizon. The sun was setting on one side, and the moon rising on the other, two different kinds of twilight at either extremity, with the snows of Etna seemingly ablaze, and a few gossamer cloudlets floating through the blueness of the firmament like snowflakes, with the smell of all that flourishing mountain vegetation, amid a solemn silence; you could see the sea in the distance, turning silver in the first glimmer of moonlight, and Catania, like a pale patch upon the shore, and the vast plain behind bound by chains of azure mountains, with the bright, winding course of the Simeto snaking across it. And then gradually, rising towards us, were all those gardens and vineyards, those villages sending us the distant sound of the angelus, and Etna's proud peak reaching towards the sky, its valleys already quite black, its snows gleaming in the last rays of sunshine, its woods rustling and murmuring and quivering. Marianna, there are times when I feel like weeping, and clasping hands with everyone around me, when I'd be incapable of uttering a single word, and my mind is crowded with thoughts . . . Honestly, I don't know how I didn't clasp hands with Signor Nino, who was standing next to me! What a crazy fool I am!

I think everyone must have felt what I was feeling, because no one spoke. Even Signor Nino, who's always cheerful, as you know, also remained silent . . .

Then we went running down the hill again, shouting and laughing, frightening the birds (who then did the same to us, by taking flight with a sudden flurry among the leaves), and playing hide-and-seek among the trees, even though our parents shouted themselves hoarse, telling us not to run. Ali and Vigilante joined in the fun, jumping and barking with joy. Here and there, amid those dark shadows, a moonbeam filtered through the branches, shedding its silvery light on the treetrunks, and casting weird shadows on the dead leaves that carpeted the ground. Signor Nino, too, no more nor less than the rest of us, ran like a child, like a madman. Two or three times, I overtook him, which left me feeling very proud. Can you imagine, beating a man! And since it was dark among the trees and he couldn't see me blush, I didn't feel embarrassed. And when I'd left all the others behind . . . including him . . . I stood there, panting, unable to catch my breath, but totally elated, and I wasn't scared of being alone in the dark, because I could hear their voices and the sound of the dogs barking . . . and, after all, Signor Nino had that splendid shot-gun slung across his shoulder.

And what a pleasure it was, too, as we came out of the woods, to be greeted by the lights of our cottage. Do you have any idea what a gladdening sight it is, in the silence and the darkness of the countryside, to see in the distance those illuminated windows, that welcoming light, which guides you, leads you, and makes you think of home, and of all the quiet joys of family life?

You can't imagine how friendly we've become with the Valentini over the past week. They're such nice people! It's as though we've been friends for decades. Annetta is a kind-hearted girl and doesn't laugh at my tunic and my strange convent ways. We're in one another's company from morning till night, going for walks, chatting, playing cards, having lunch together, and sometimes dinner as well. Would you believe that I've learned to play cards, too? For heaven's sake, don't tell anyone! Though I'm not very good yet, and I nearly always lose, Signor Nino is always ready to help me, to offer his advice and guidance, and he doesn't mind not playing himself. When I go back to the convent, I promise you, I'll forget all about card games.

My God, the convent! That's the only cloud darkening these bright horizons. But let's not think about that right now, Marianna, let's be cheerful and happy, and let God's will be done!

And while we're here, enjoying ourselves, safe and untroubled, and out of harm's way, think of all those poor people grieving and suffering! all that misery! all those tears! all those victims! The news that reaches us here, every four or five days, is very sad. May God have mercy on the many who are afflicted!

There are such fears and apprehensions! The peasants here believe in poisoners, in poisonous rays, and heaven knows what else . . . Poor wretches! They're like me, when I'm afraid, I see ghosts! That's why every night, in the valleys, on the mountains, all around, you see flares and torches, and you hear the continual sound of gunfire, as though they were trying to scare off cunning wolves, or human savages! It's sad, but at night, in the darkness and the silence, amid this general tumult, it's also terrifying.

Now I'm sad too, aren't I? And only a moment ago I was happy, telling you how we've been enjoying ourselves. You say that you're having fun too, and that you're in good company. I believe you, but I bet it's not as good as ours. You also say that you won't be returning to the convent – lucky you! But that means I'll have to go back without you! Right now, I want to be happy. God will take care of the future! Carino is better – he's grown much bigger, and even a little naughty. He's lively, chirpy and bright, and he has such a loud voice! If I let him, I think he'd be fearless enough to stand up to the cat. Poor Vigilante was given such a nasty beating by the steward that he came yelping to tell me his troubles. I petted him, and I've always some tasty titbit to give him, and now he remains at the door of my room.

I don't think there's anything I've forgotten to tell you. Write me a long letter soon. Tell me that you love me, and send your love as well to my friend Annetta, who sends you hers.

Goodbye, goodbye, goodbye.

If you knew, Marianna, if you only knew . . . The terrible sin I've committed . . . My God! How am I going to summon up the courage to tell you? Don't tell me off! I'll confess to no one else but you – but only in a whisper, mind, and all in a fluster . . . Don't look me in the face! Hold me tight and listen.

I've been dancing! Can you imagine? I've been dancing! But listen . . . don't shout at me! There was no one watching – only papa, Giuditta, Gigi, mama, Annetta, the Valentini . . . and Signor Nino . . . In fact, he was the one I danced with . . . Listen, I'll explain . . . you'll see that it wasn't my fault . . . I wasn't to blame . . . they forced me . . .

Yesterday evening the Valentini brought their harmonium. Annetta played, and then Giuditta. Everyone was dancing – Annetta, Giuditta, and even Gigi a little. My sister's bed had to be dismantled to make room for a dance floor. After Giuditta had finished dancing, Signor Nino came and invited me. I felt my face burning, and I wished I were a hundred feet below the ground. I stammered, not knowing what to say. I refused, repeatedly, I swear to you. Everyone was laughing and clapping. Papa came and took me by the hand. He gave me a hug and said there was no great harm in my dancing as well, and he too was laughing. It was no use my trying to explain I didn't even know how to dance, I hadn't been taught that either at the convent. Signor Nino volunteered to teach me. I couldn't see clearly any more, I felt dizzy, my ears were ringing, and my legs were trembling. I let myself be led, I let myself be dragged along, without the least idea of what they were doing with me. It was excruciating, Marianna . . . Yet, when he took me by the hand.. when he put his arm around my waist . . . it seemed to me that his hand was hot, that every vein of my blood was on fire, and that an icy chill was flooding into my heart! But at the same time I felt comforted. My heart was pounding, feeling that other heart beating against it. Everyone must have been laughing at me. You're laughing, too. Even I can laugh at myself now. How many young women of our age have not danced a dozen times at least? I wonder whether at first they went through the same experience as I did? But afterwards I confess that the music, those happy faces, the words of encouragement he whispered in my ear, his hand that held mine almost dispelled my confusion, even shame . . . Poor Marianna, don't be cross with me. I very nearly felt happy . . .

My dear Marianna, forgive me! I shan't do it again. Anyway, I hope they leave me alone now. They've made enough fun of my tunic and my awkwardness . . . including him . . . Signor Nino . . . But no! I'm sure he didn't want to make me dance just to laugh at me . . . He meant to please me . . . and in fact he was being too kind to me, to a poor postulant who didn't know how to move, who stumbled at every step, and was overcome with dizziness . . . and he dances so well! If you'd seen him dancing with Giuditta – she certainly knows how to dance!

Afterwards we played a little music. Annetta and Giuditta sang a few theatrical songs. Then they absolutely insisted that I sang as well . . . Tell me, what on earth could I have sung, apart from *Salve Regina*? Well, they said they'd even settle for *Salve Regina*. They were surely trying to tease me by making me sing, and my papa most of all! In the choir, as you well know, we sing almost in darkness, behind screens, with a veil over our face, among those that we know very well. But to sing in public, in front of so many people! Signor Nino was there, too! Yet I was obliged to sing – not the words, mind, only the tune. My voice was quavering, and I could hardly breathe, but they were very kind and didn't laugh, in fact they applauded. Apparently they thought the music of *Salva Regina* was really beautiful. I could see that Signor Nino was very touched by it. And the way he was looking at me, when he's usually so cheerful and light-hearted.

I've told you everything that I've been doing, and thinking, and all the fun I've been having, and all the terrible sins I've committed, even at the risk of being lectured by you. I wouldn't have dared to confess them to our saintly old chaplain ... but if I didn't tell you everything, my dearest sister, if I didn't open my heart to you, and confide in you, I think all these things would oppress me. I need to have a long chat with you about them, to recall all the details, to ponder over them, and to talk to myself about them, to see them written down on paper, to dream about them ... There are moments when all these thoughts are seething in my mind, making me feel dizzy, befuddled and dazed.

I'm mad. These new sensations must be too violent for me, after the peace and quiet of the convent that I'm used to. I'm glad to be able to talk about them to you at least, and to share with you what I cannot contain in my own heart.

Write to me, write soon. Don't take too long to reply. Comfort me, talk to your poor friend who's troubled and perturbed by all this disturbance and novelty, and all these new impressions, and who trembles like a little bird, frightened even by curious onlookers who certainly have no intention of hurting it, but do so just by gathering round to watch.

I want to cry, and laugh, and sing, I want to be happy. I need a letter from you. I need to talk to you, do you understand? Hug me, Marianna ... If only I could weep and bury my face in your shoulder!

Thursday was a lovely day! It was papa's name-day! I don't need to tell you that everyone in our little family was up at dawn, and our little house was filled with joy and happiness. Mama had already had a turkey's neck wrung, and was supervising preparations for the meal. Giuditta gave my father a beautiful silk cap, which she'd embroidered in secret as a surprise. I could only give a bunch of wild flowers I picked at daybreak and that were still wet with dew. It was a very humble little posy, but my dear kind papa was just as pleased with my present as he was with my sister's, and he hugged us both with tears in his eyes. Our friends arrived as soon as it was light, preceded by cheerful cries, shots fired into the air, and Ali's barking. What festiveness! The Valentini, too, brought flowers, but real garden flowers that they had ordered specially from Viagrande. My poor little bunch looked very modest beside those splendid blooms. They also gave us a fine hare killed the day before. Signor Valentini never goes hunting, but his son does ... Mama appreciated the hare more than the flowers. And I confess that in the past few days I've become almost reconciled with hunters ... It must be a matter of getting used to them ... And what can we women possibly understand of pastimes like these that men take such pleasure in? Papa invited our friends to eat with us. It was a wonderful day! Everyone was very good-humoured, and they all sang, and laughed, and even danced – I didn't, mind you.

After the meal, we went for our usual walk. It was a beautiful evening. But I don't know why, I wasn't as bright and cheerful as everyone else, and as I'd been before. I liked hearing the quiet rustle of falling leaves, the sighing of the trees, the distant call of a barn owl, I liked feeling scared in the darkest shadows and being on my own, away from the others, and tears gradually misted my eyes.

What is the mystery inside us, Marianna? I should have

been so happy that day, when everyone else was. I can't explain this strangeness even to myself. It's probably my funny little brain that's more suited to the quietness of the convent, and feeling out of place here is unsettled and disturbed, and even a little crazy.

Goodbye for now. I'll write again soon. This is a short, even skimpy, letter, although I ought to be sending a nice long one telling you lots more – all the foolish things that pass through my mind, all the things that I can't chat to you about face to face. But what can I say? I haven't the heart for it today. I feel tired and listless, and my thoughts are confused. Till tomorrow then.

You must be cross with me for not having replied to your letter, and you're right to be, Marianna, but I'm already cross with myself. I don't know what's wrong with me, I just don't know ... The smallest task, the least activity makes me tired ... Go ahead and scold me ... I'm a real lazy-bones. I wish I could spend all day long sitting in the shade of the chestnut trees, and all night staring up at the sky. Everything that had most charm now bores me. I no longer have any desire to go for walks in the chestnut grove, or to sing, I can't laugh any more – everything irritates me. Your poor friend Maria is feeling very sad! Even I don't know why. Perhaps the Good Lord wanted to show me how transient are the joys and pleasures that don't belong to life inside the convent. Oh God, there are moments when I'm almost afraid of myself ... because even my prayers are distracted ... God, forgive me, and comfort me! God, sustain me!

Carino has almost ceased to be tame, because for many days now I haven't been playing with him any more. He flies away from me! Have I really become so disagreeable? Vigilante doesn't show me the same affection that he used to, because I don't pay attention to him, and he realizes that he's being a nuisance.

Do you think I could be ill, Marianna? Between you and me, I almost wish I were ill, because then there'd be a reason for all this boredom and tiredness, and they wouldn't frighten me.

But you're well, and happy, and light-hearted – you must write to me, write often. Love me a hundred times better, because I'm in more need of your love and you're much dearer to me now, and the only sweet feeling left to me is a great fondness for my loved ones, for everyone I know, and as you can imagine, for you too!

I'm convinced, Marianna, that all this worldly tumult, all these powerful sensations, and these pleasures are extremely bad for us poor, weak, faint-hearted souls. We're humble little flowers accustomed to the gentle protection of the hothouse, and destroyed by fresh air.

Do you remember when I wrote to you two months ago and told you how bright and cheerful I felt? How avid for joy my heart was, and how it treasured every new emotion? How I thanked the good Lord and praised him for all these wonderful sensations that my heart was opening up to? It's true, Marianna! Alas, it's true what the nuns kept telling us, and what Father Anselmo said repeatedly from the pulpit: that the real, lasting joys are the calm, serene joys of the convent. I can't explain why, but the joys of the world are not always the same. I know from experience . . . I feel so differently now! Everything makes me feel tired, oppresses me, and bothers me . . . I find everything a cause of unease, and anxiety . . . and even dismay. I'm scared by the very fact that I can't account for the sudden fits of insane, almost delirious joy and for the unpredictable sadnesses that overwhelm me. I feel unhappy among all these gifts from the Creator for which I once used to glorify Him . . .

I wish I could return within those blessed convent walls. I wish I could kneel in the chancel and cling to the feet of Jesus on that cross. I wish I could kiss you, and bury my face on your shoulder, and shed the tears gathered in my heart.

Don't laugh at me, Marianna, pity me instead. Pity me, because I feel so sad, and I can't understand my sadness, I don't know the reason for it – maybe I'm wicked and ungrateful to the good Lord who has showered so many blessings on me; ungrateful to my dear papa who tries to dispel my sadness with countless endearments; ungrateful to my family and friends . . .

I can't write any more. I feel like crying. I've spent nearly all night long at the window, staring into the intense darkness, which seemed to me full of ghosts, and listening to the distant sound of the dogs whining, and the drone of nocturnal insects . . . and I wasn't afraid!

If only I could throw my arms around you and weep! I wish you'd write! Write to me! That's all I can say.

My dear Marianna, you say that you're worried about me, about my state of mind. You ask lots of questions that make no sense to me, embarrassing questions that I don't know how to answer. You want countless explanations for things I don't understand myself. If you were here, if we could confide in each other, arm in arm, under the trees, in the deepest shade, perhaps you – being a young lady now, who won't be going back to the convent again, and have some experience of the world – perhaps you might be able to answer my questions and resolve my doubts; you could comfort and reassure me. But what I can tell you?

Even your questions worry and disturb me ... Why do you ask the reason for my not having mentioned the Valentini in the letters that I've written recently, which have been so dejected, whereas I used to tell you so much about them in my earlier letters, which were so cheerful. Why have you pointed out that while Signor Nino's name crops up repeatedly at first, it seems to have been carefully avoided latterly? How did you notice? I wasn't aware of it myself ... And, God knows, I couldn't tell you why! But you're right, and you've made me realize that even now it's taken a great effort to write that name ... And you've probably noticed that my hand was trembling ... And if you could see my face!

Now, I'll tell everything ... I'll place my heart in your hands. You'll be better than me at interrogating and analysing it, for I haven't any idea ... You can tell me what I must do to overcome this illness that's afflicting me, and how to return to being light-hearted and carefree and happy. You'll open your arms to me ...

I don't know what's troubling me, but it must be something bad, because I've been reluctant to confide in you, I feel almost guilty, and I'm overcome with shame, anxiety, an inexplicable fear, as if I had some secret to hide from everybody, and everyone were staring at me trying to discover it.

What is that secret? My God, even I couldn't say . . . I'll tell you everything, everything! If you can detect it, you must tell me, and I promise to master it, if it's a wickedness or temptation. I promise to be good, and pray to God to give me strength and enlightenment, to help me . . .

I've analysed everything myself to see what this wickedness might be, where this trouble might stem from. I've examined all my feelings, and thoughts, and even the way I've been spending my time, the people I speak to, the things I see . . . I can't find anything, except . . . But you'll think I'm mad, and laugh at me.

When I've written before I've told you that we've become very close friends with the Valentini. Annetta is like another Marianna to me . . . But you've made me think that her brother has a certain effect on me . . . It's true: I'd almost say that he frightens me.

No, I'm not being nasty, Marianna! Don't blame me for it! It's just some eccentricity, some foolishness, I'm sure. I realize that it's wrong of me, and I try not to let it get the better of me . . . because he's such a kind young man, and always so considerate towards me . . . But I can't explain the feeling he produces in me . . . It's not dislike or hostility . . . and yet I'm afraid of him . . . and every time I meet him I blush, and turn pale, I tremble, and wish I could escape.

But then he talks to me, I listen, and stay with him . . . I don't know why . . . I feel unable to separate myself from him . . . and I think of Father Anselmo, talking to us from the pulpit about the lure of the evil spirit, and I'm scared . . .

My God! I'm not saying that they're the same thing . . . It's just a comparison. I wish I could explain to you the effect he has on me . . ..

He's very polite to everyone, though, including me . . . and I'm not rude to him, I swear! I'm grateful for his tact and kindness . . .

When we happened to find ourselves alone the other day, after the famous dance, he said to me, 'Thank you, signorina.'

'What for?'

'For being good enough to dance with me. If you only knew how happy it made me!'

And he said this in such a way that I felt completely disconcerted. My God, how men exaggerate their compliments! But I don't know why he said this in a very low voice, and I thought he even blushed . . . and perhaps that's why I blushed, too . . . and I didn't know what to reply . . .

You see how thoughtful he can be, to please me. Another time he said to me, 'How well that tunic suits you!' That's what he said! My ugly black tunic! I couldn't explain why, but I think I felt very pleased. I reddened and stammered and didn't know where to put myself.

You'll say that I'm mad, and you're right, because it certainly can't be his good manners that so disturb me.

So why am I embarrassed whenever I hear his voice? When I find him staring at me, why do I suddenly feel the blood rushing to my face, and a kind of shiver in my heart?

Do you know, Marianna, I think I've found the explanation for all this. In the convent we've been taught to think of men in general and young men in particular in such a way that we can't encounter one without being thrown into complete confusion. For why is it that my sister, Giuditta, who, after all, is younger than me, never feels in the least embarrassed talking to him? Why on the contrary can she laugh and joke and have long, frank talks with him, without blushing, whereas I think I'd die if I had to do the same? And yet . . . God forgive me . . . I think that because of this I sometimes have a feeling towards my sister that resembles jealousy . . .

O God! Call me back to you, in the convent, where there is peace, silence and composure. Calm my spirit and illuminate my mind!

On Monday I met him in the chestnut grove. Fortunately, Gigi was with me. He had his shot-gun over his shoulder, and we heard him singing to himself long before he became aware of our presence. You don't know what a sweet voice he has! I recognized it immediately: my heart felt as though it would burst from my breast, and I wanted to run away, to escape, because of that same old ridiculous fluster . . . His dog, Ali, saw us first, and came running up to us, barking joyfully. So, really and truly, we had to stay . . . although I'd turned scarlet and was trembling all over . . . He must have noticed my agitation. He came up and held out his hand. I had to give him mine, for it's customary here to shake hands, even with men, which doesn't seem right to me . . . he was bound to realize that my poor hand was trembling.

To return home, we had to go through the densest part of the wood, and on the edge of it, which is very rocky, there were a lot of briars and brambles. He wanted to accompany me and lend me his arm. I was trembling so much that he said, 'Lean on me properly, signorina, you're stumbling at every step.'

This was true. We went quite a long way in silence, and as we walked, I kicked the dry leaves lying on the ground, so that he couldn't hear the beating of my heart. He must have taken pity on my embarrassment, because he tried to break the silence by saying, 'What a lovely day! What a pleasant walk it's been!' And he sighed . . . Actually, Gigi complained that I was treading on his heels . . . Then we sat on a low wall by the vineyard, and he settled himself beside me. All I could see was the butt of his gun, casting bizarre shadows on the ground. Ali came and rested his big head on my lap, laughing at me with his beautiful, vivacious eyes. I stroked him, and he showed his thanks by wagging his tail. His master said to me, 'You see how affectionate towards you Ali is? Don't you love him?'

I don't know why this very innocent question completely flustered me, and I felt that I loved poor Ali immensely. And he, too, stroked his dog . . . and then our hands met, and I felt that mine was trembling. My own silence embarrassed me. I tried to think of a reply, and all I could stammer out was, 'You have such a fine dog, signor!'

He didn't say anything else, and sighed. Why did he sigh? He must have felt unhappy, too, poor thing! In fact, I thought he'd been looking more dispirited in the last few days . . . and that moment when he sighed, I felt a great tenderness towards him, and no longer my usual dismay, but such an amicable feeling that I wished I were a man like him, a friend of his, or a brother, so that I could throw my arms around his neck and ask him what was wrong, so that I could comfort him, or at least share his troubles with him.

Oh, yes! these are terrible sins! And imagine how painful it will be to confess them! And I have an even greater sin on my conscience . . . a keen desire to know what was making him so sad . . . We women are so curious . . . But of course I daredn't ask him.

Since then I've seen him only in the evening, with his family. I don't venture out on my own any more. I sew idly at my window, and every day that I hear his voice, or hear him whistling for his dog, up in the woods, or that I see a figure moving swiftly through the clumps of trees in the distance, my heart beats the way it did when we sat beside each other in silence, with our hands resting on that fine dog's head.

Every time I meet him, I feel the same confusion, and so I try to avoid any encounter. But there are times when I can't escape, you see . . . and I have to hide my discomfort and stay. When he looks at me, my heart leaps, and I wish I could die to hide my blushes. I feel as though all eyes are fixed on me, wondering why I'm blushing . . . and I . . . O God! I couldn't say . . . I don't know! But I take the first chance I can to seek refuge in my little room and bury my burning face in my pillows, and cry . . . I don't know why but crying seems to make me feel better and relieve me of a great burden.

But the day before yesterday, as I was drying my eyes, I saw a figure at the window. It was him – with his elbows resting on the windowsill, with his face cupped in his hands. You can imagine how I felt! He was also very agitated. He tried to smile, and it was such a sad smile that I thought he was weeping. Then he stammered, 'Why do you keep running away, signorina?' I wished the ground would open up and swallow me. Fortunately my sister appeared. It cost me an extraordinary effort to calm myself, or rather to force my face to lie, and I went out and joined the rest of the party, who were enjoying themselves out on the lawn. Giuditta was with him, talking and laughing, at her ease – she wasn't trembling!

Oh, the convent, the convent! That's what I need, that's the place for me. Outside there's nothing but confusion and dismay.

You see . . . they'll think I'm ill-mannered . . . he most of all! God, who can read my heart, knows I'm not like that, and that I'm not to blame if my shyness and the way of life I'm used to, which is very different from theirs, make me seem so! But who's going to believe me? Yesterday, as everyone was coming back indoors, because the evening coolness had turned chilly, he came up to me, looking sad and pale, and took my hand. I was trembling so much that I couldn't draw it back. I was in a daze . . . He said in his gentlest voice, 'What have I ever done to you, signorina? Why do keep avoiding me?'

My God! My God! I wanted to throw myself at his feet and ask his forgiveness, and to tell him that he was mistaken, that it wasn't my fault . . . I don't know what I said, or stammered. Annetta came up and I threw myself in her arms and burst into tears.

My dear Marianna, try to be of comfort to me, and help me! Even you're abandoning me! I'm alone, sad and unhappy. Pray God that I may soon return to my tranquil, modest existence, and that the world's stormy blast, which has sown tumult in my dismayed soul, may be stilled in the silence of those corridors.

I've been writing to you with tears clouding my eyes. I don't even know what I've written. Forgive me, and love me, for I desperately need to be loved.

The other evening, when I came into the room where my family and the Valentini were gathered, I was so upset after what he'd said to me that everyone noticed. My stepmother made a scene: she told me off for being ill-mannered, and wilful, and for indulging in irrational fits of joy and bouts of gloom. My father tried to defend me, by saying that I was unwell.

Everyone else remained silent. This torture went on for half an hour. When I was able to retreat to my room, I thanked the Lord and prayed ardently that He would call me to Him.

I had a dreadful night, without so much as closing my eyes. I've searched my heart, and I'm scared.

Marianna, if I weren't afraid of committing a sin and causing grief to my father, Giuditta, my brother, and you ... to everyone who loves me ... I'd wish to die of cholera ...

Goodbye.

20 November

Marianna! Marianna! I love him! I love him! For pity's sake, don't regard me with contempt. I'm terribly unhappy. Forgive me!

O God! Why so harsh a punishment? Now I'm blaspheming! O God, how I've cried! Is there any woman more wretched than I am?

I love him! What a horrible thing to say – it's a sin, a crime, but it's no use my pretending otherwise. My sin is stronger than me. I've tried to escape, and it has clung to me, it has pinned me down, and trampled my face in the mire. My whole being is replete with that man – my head, my heart, my blood. I see him before my eyes as I write to you, in my dreams, and in my prayers. I can't think of anything else. I feel as if his name is always on my lips, and that every word I utter turns into the name by which he's called. When I hear him, I feel happy. When he looks at me, I tremble. I wish I could always be with him, and yet I avoid him. I wish I could die for him. Everything I feel for that man is new, unfamiliar and terrifying . . . more fervent than the love I bear my father, and more intense than my love for God. This is what, in the world, is called 'love'. I've experienced it, I've seen it . . . it's horrible! horrible! It's God's punishment, damnation, blasphemy! Marianna, I'm lost! Marianna, pray for me.

Yesterday, he'd gone to Catania on some family business. He was supposed to catch the coach back to Trecastagne and be home before nightfall, but at nine o'clock there was still no sign of him. You can imagine how upset his family and all the rest of us were! The reports we get these days are so bleak, there wasn't a soul among us who didn't imagine the worst. His mother and Annetta were crying. Signor Valentini was extremely restless and kept climbing up the bank that rises above the vineyard, from which you can see a good stretch of the lane leading to the village, for his son was supposed to have got off the coach at the usual stop and then walked up here. It was very dark, and you couldn't see more than ten yards down the lane. Two messengers had been sent off to try and find out the reason for this delay, and to let us know if he was on his way. Every so often, his poor father called out his name, as if hoping that he would respond from a distance. You can imagine how anxiously we all strained our ears: one minute went by, then ten, and his voice died away, far off down the valley, and was followed by silence. The clock struck nine thirty, then ten! There was general weeping and wailing. Signor Valentini had gone out alone, in the dark, like a madman, to make inquiries of every passer-by, determined not to give up until he had found his son. But there wasn't a soul to be seen. Not even the boldest traveller would have ventured out at that hour of the night, when the roads were under the suspicious watch of peasant-folk on their guard against cholera! Those tears broke my heart. That silence terrified me. That darkness seemed full of horrible visions. I'd shut myself in my bedroom, to kneel at the foot of the cross and weep, and to pray for him. Now and again, I'd interrupt my prayers, dry my tears, and stifle my sobs in order to strain my ears, to devote all my attention to listening. Outside all you could hear in the distance was the sound of a few gunshots that threw us all into crisis, and the lugubrious howling of the dogs. I became superstitious. I thought, 'After I've said one hundred Hail Marys, I'll hear his voice.' I said fifty straight off, then I began to recite the rest more slowly, because I felt that I'd said the first ones in too much of a rush, that it was cheating on the time that I'd set, that God would answer my prayers because I'd said my Hail Marys too distractedly. When I had recited the last ten, I went back and started all over again, deluding myself that I'd miscounted . . . I said the last two, one after the other, breaking off to listen . . . And I thought I heard distant voices . . . I waited, and waited . . . nothing! silence! Then I said to myself, 'If the first person to speak is Annetta, he'll arrive in a quarter of an hour . . .' Then, 'By the time the wind has made the leaves on the trees rustle ten times, he'll be here.'

The branches tossed and stirred, and no one came! Then I felt as if I were suffocating, and losing my mind, and the blood were flowing so fast through all my veins that it was making me run about aimlessly like a madwoman. The room felt cramped and the roof seemed to be pressing down on me. I went out on to the lawn. It upset me to see his poor relatives weeping, listening anxiously to the slightest sounds of the countryside, and quietly voicing false hopes, to delude themselves more than anyone else. I went and sat on the wall, away from everybody, in the darkness. With burning eyes, I stared into the shadows, almost feeling that I could dispel them by the strength of my desire, listening to the howling of dogs in the distance and trying to tell whether they were barking at his approach.

O God! what agony! All of a sudden my heart seemed to stop beating . . . I heard a distant bark, a bark I recognized. My heart began to pound furiously, making a noise when all I wanted was to listen . . . It was nothing, nothing! I was mistaken . . . Then came another bark, closer and more distinct. This time everyone heard it: it was Ali barking. He's here! He's coming! That's Ali's bark! Ah!

Ali raced closer, barking joyfully, announcing the good news at the top of his voice. He knew that we were worried and frightened, and he came running . . . you could hear the vines suddenly shake as he raced past. He still hadn't come into view, but I could have said exactly where he was. My heart felt as though it would burst from my breast. Everyone had come rushing up to the wall, beside me.

Here he is. He jumps up on the wall. It's Ali! It's him! He leaps on me, barking with joy, although panting, and poor Ali, he also is overwrought.

I hugged him, extremely tightly, because I thought I was going to faint, and I burst into tears.

When poor Nino arrived, he was pale, tired and breathless! He'd walked from Catania, because the coach had left without him, and he hadn't been able to find any other carriage prepared to make the journey at that hour. His father, who'd come back with him, kissed him. His mother and Annetta held him in their arms. Everyone made a fuss of him; everyone cried with joy. He must have thought me selfish and disagreeable, because I ran off and shut myself in my room, to cry, and laugh, and sob without restraint, to embrace the foot of the cross, the furniture and the walls!

O God! Is there any creature on earth more wretched than me?

Since this temptation has taken possession of me, I don't recognize myself any more. My eyes see more clearly, my mind learns of mysteries that should have remained unknown to me for ever. My heart experiences new sentiments that it should never have experienced, that it ought never to have been allowed to experience. It's happy, it feels closer to God, it cries, it feels small, alone, and weak. This is all frightful! On top of which, insignificant trifles become a torment: a look, a gesture, a tone of voice, a step; whether he sits in one place or another; whether he talks to this person or that. You won't understand, you'll think I'm mad. O God! If only I were, how happy I would be! This is to experience constant doubt, anxiety, dismay, and indescribable delight. Add to all this, the thought of what my status is, remorse for my sin, my powerlessness to fight against a feeling that is stronger than me, that has seized me, consumes me, overwhelms me, and makes me happy by subjugating me . . . the desolation of discovering my lowliness, discovering what I am – I'm less than a woman, I'm a poor nun, with a faint heart for everything that falls outside the confines of the convent, and the immensity of this horizon that is unexpectedly opening up before her, blinds and bewilders her.

I wonder whether this love, this sin, this monstrousness is not an aspect of God! I want to be beautiful, like the feeling I have inside me. I look at myself, surprised by my own unusual curiosity, and I'm saddened by what I find myself to be: a shapeless bundle of black twill, with hair unattractively scraped back, and unrefined manners, a shyness that might seem awkward ... and I see other young girls around me, who are elegant and gracious, and commit no sin by being in love, like me ... I blush for myself, I blush for my blushes ...

And yet ... that's not all! There's another cross to bear: the fear that this secret, which I jealously keep to myself, will be discovered! It means being afraid of your blushes, your pallor, the trembling of your voice, the beating of your heart! It means having the impression that your entire being is accusing you, that everyone is spying on you ... and feeling ready to die of shame if this disaster should occur! I blush at what I'm writing to you, at what you will read ... you who are a part of me!... and I impose it on myself as a form of penance ... I'm so madly in love with him, and I'd die of shame if he knew!

I wish I could throw my arms around his neck, I wish I could die at his feet, but not for all the gold in the world would I dare to give him my hand. And if he looks at me, I lower my eyes. And to think that in any case my father ... my stepmother ... he, too ... might be able to see into my heart! O God! let me sooner die!

And if I were to tell you that this fear of mine is not completely unfounded ... that this morning my stepmother called me, and fixing me with a gaze that seemed to penetrate right through to my heart, she said, 'You've been much too pale and restless for some time now. What's wrong with you?'

I was quaking, and I've no idea what I stammered out, but I didn't know what to say. She went on, looking at me in that same unnerving way: 'I've noticed a great change in you in recent days. My child, if the country air doesn't agree with you, your father won't insist on keeping you here – he'll let you return to your convent.' And she accompanied these few words with such a look and such a tone of voice that seemed to say, 'I know everything. I know your secret.'

I felt like dying. Fortunately, I was sitting down, otherwise I'd have fallen to the ground, and she didn't notice that my eyes filled with tears, because at that moment Giuditta came in, looking very happy. Oh, my poor mama, lying at rest in Camposanto . . . if only I could have thrown myself in your arms and, bursting into tears, asked your forgiveness!

Giuditta said, 'Listen, mama: the Valentini have invited us to go with them to the Bertoni's house – they live just near by. There'll be dancing, you know! Come on, now, mama, be a darling! Do let's go . . . What fun a dance in the country will be!' And the dear girl cajoled her mother so sweetly that her stern expression immediately softened. She kissed Giuditta with a smile, and said just one word: 'Flibbertigibbet!'

Oh, how blessed is a mother's holy love, entirely revealed in a single word or caress! How blessed is the happiness which the happiness of our dear ones gives us! They both seemed so beautiful to me just then, in the blessings that Heaven had showered on them, that I prayed to God for all those, like me, who are deprived of them.

Giuditta hurried away to get ready, skipping and singing to herself, and she called for me to do her hair. She has wonderful chestnut braids. And every day, when I loosen her hair to comb it, I think what a great shame it would be if they were condemned to being cut off like mine. However, that day I was in such turmoil that I couldn't do anything right. I braided her hair twenty times, but she was never satisfied, and kept angrily undoing her braids.

'My God!' she exclaimed. 'Anyone would think you were doing it deliberately today!'

'I'm sorry,' I said, 'it's not my fault.'

'No, it's probably that you're tired of combing my hair.'

'Oh, what ever do you mean, Giuditta! No, I swear I'm not. I'm doing my best,' I replied tearfully.

My dear sister is infinitely kind. She looked at me in

surprise, shrugged her shoulders, took the comb from my hand, and said, 'Go on, there's no reason to cry. I'll do it myself.'

I wanted to hug her, to kiss her, to ask her forgiveness, to get rid of that knot of bitterness that I felt here, in my heart. How stupid and troublesome I am! It was already late, and she was keeping everyone waiting. She was right to lose patience and say to me, 'Oh, for heaven's sake, leave me to comb my hair by myself at least!'

So I went out, wiping my eyes. Annetta met me at the door, and said, 'What are you doing? Aren't you coming, too?'

'What can you be thinking of?' exclaimed my step-mother. 'A postulant! That would be the limit!'

Nino kept staring at me and didn't say anything. I could see him, even though I wasn't looking at him. Meanwhile, my father came up and asked what all these preparations were for, and the reason for this merriment. 'What about you?' he then asked.

'I'm staying at home, papa.'

'No, you can come with us – we're in the country, after all.'

'Papa, I'd rather stay at home.'

'Then I'll stay behind with you.' (Dear papa! He really does love me!)

'What? Then who'll accompany us?' said his wife.

'You can go with our friends here.'

'But it's not good manners, the first time that we're to visit people we don't know. Maria can perfectly well stay behind with the maid and the steward for company.'

There was some further discussion, but papa eventually conceded to his wife's wishes – because, you know, my poor papa never contradicts her, for the sake of peace.

My friend, I confess that for the first time in my life, I was sorry to be the only one left out, when everyone was so looking forward to having a good time . . . And shall I tell you something else? There was another thing that upset me . . . the idea that he would be seeing so many other

71

pretty young girls, and that he would even dance with them. At the thought of this, my heart filled with tears . . .

Now I'm alone. I watched them go off, in high spirits, singing. Only he looked sad. He gazed at me as if he would like to have asked me a hundred questions. He gave his arm to my sister . . . How beautiful Giuditta was in her lovely pale-blue dress, leaning on his arm, laughing and chatting with him.

I followed them with my eyes until they turned into the lane, and disappeared behind the hawthorn hedge that rises above the vineyard wall. Then for a while I could still hear their voices and their laughter, a merriment that was painful to me . . . O God, what an envious and wicked person I am! I had to think of him to prevent myself from sobbing. I had to remember the way he stared at me, in order not to envy them . . .

I was left on my own. The stars began to shine. It was a beautiful autumn evening, still mild and warm . . .

The steward's wife has lit the fire to cook their soup, and placed her baby in its cradle. Her husband has come home from the vineyard, leaving his gun at the door, and started playing with his little boy, who stands between his knees. All is calm, peaceful and serene. Only I am anxious, sad and unhappy.

I'm writing down everything that's close to my heart, and when my tears prevent me from being able to see what I'm writing any more, I look out of my window at the starry sky and the shadow of the trees. I think of that party, and of all those happy people enjoying themselves, with him! I think of him! And then I can't write any more, I've no other thoughts but for him alone. I have to picture him, in my mind's eye at least, while he's there dancing and laughing with someone else . . .

I'll say goodbye now . . .

Marianna! Marianna! Cry with me! Laugh with me! Hug me! He loves me! Would you believe it! He loves me! Can you imagine! I can't tell you any more. You'll understand totally what these three little words mean: he loves me!

Yesterday evening, do you remember? I had that sad letter in front of me, with my elbows resting on the desk. My tears were very quietly falling on to the paper and, without my noticing, were blotting out what I had written. All of a sudden came a noise from outside . . . the sound of footsteps! Could you explain why the sound of footsteps should be detected by your heart, as though the heart could hear? And why it should shake your nerves, and make your blood run cold?

I looked up . . . the window was open, and outside there was a figure, a voice softly calling me. It was him, do you understand? Him! If a cry didn't escape me, it was because I couldn't breathe.

'Forgive me, signorina,' he said, 'forgive me.' And that was all.

I dared not look at him, but those words were as sweet as honey to my heart.

'Your mother's mean and unfair to you. Everyone over there is having fun, and I thought of you, being here on your own . . . Have I done wrong?' After a brief pause, during which he must have heard my heart beating, he added, 'Will you forgive me?'

Then I looked up at him, and I saw him with his elbows resting on the windowsill and his chin cupped in his hands, as I had seen him before. He had been thinking of me, and his voice was trembling!

'Signor!' I said. 'Signor!' And I couldn't say anything else. Then he began to sigh, in the same way that I did. 'Listen, Maria . . .' he said, but nothing else. He passed his hand over his eyes, and seemed to be stammering – he, a man! I was shaking all over, as if that name had penetrated every pore of my living flesh. He called me Maria, do you understand? Why did it have that effect on me, to hear him say my name?

'Listen,' he repeated. 'You're a victim.'

'Oh no, signor!'

'Yes, you're a victim of your circumstances, your step-mother's unkindness, your father's weakness, and fate!'

'No, signor, no.'

'Then why are you forced to become a nun?'

'No one's forced me, signor . . . it was my own free will.'

'Ah!' And he sighed again. I think he actually wiped his eyes. I couldn't see him clearly, because he was in the dark, in front of the window, and my eyes were veiled with tears.

'Necessity,' I said.

He didn't say anything. Then after a few moments' silence, he asked me – but his voice was husky – 'And will you return to the convent?'

I hesitated, but replied, 'Yes.'

He fell silent again. He didn't say any more. Then I waited. I waited for a long time for him to say something. I wiped my eyes to see if he'd gone: he was still there, in the same place, in the same position, except that his face was buried in his hands. This gave me courage, and I stepped forward, away from the candlelight that was bother-ing me. You know how narrow my little room is – one step and you're by the window . . . He heard me and raised his head, and I saw that he was crying. He held out his hand to me, without a word. There was a moment when I couldn't see anything at all any more, either with my own eyes or in mind's eye, and I found myself with my hands in his.

'Maria,' he said, 'why are you going to return to the convent?'

'Do you think I know? I must. I was born a nun.'

'So you'll leave me then?' And he wept silently, like a child, without the pride that other men have to hide their

74

tears. I think I must have cried too, because I discovered that my cheeks were wet, and my hands as well ... but my hands might have been wet with his tears, which I felt dripping on them. In fact, when I was alone again, locked in my room ... tell me off and shout at me, if you want to ... I kissed my hands while they were still damp.

We stayed like that, in silence, for a long time. The only thing he said was, 'How happy I am!'

'And I,' I replied, almost without being aware of it.

You see, Marianna, we were crying and saying that we were happy! But we hadn't yet said that we loved each other. Such sweetness flooded my heart that I wasn't thinking of anything any more, and I no longer felt ashamed to be with a man ... with him ... alone, at night! We didn't speak, and didn't look at each other. We gazed up at the sky, and it was as though our spirits communed through the surface of our hands, and embraced each other in the meeting of our gazes among the stars.

Marianna, this part of God that has been given to mankind must be very great if everything before it – both sin and crime, duties and the most sacred attachments – pales into insignificance, if it can create a paradise out of a single word!

I'll leave you now. My heart's too full to think of anything else. In writing to you, I've relived the same emotions ... Now I need to be alone, to dream, think and be happy ...

How wretched we are, my friend, if we can't be the judges of our own happiness. I wrote you a letter that today is a bitter irony, that I can't read without crying. Listen: there we were, at the window, silent and happy, with our dreams. All of a sudden there was uproar: Vigilante was barking, and my father's voice could be heard, as well as Gigi's. I abruptly drew back and closed the window. I was trembling all over, as if I'd committed a great offence. Papa found me in bed. I was running a fever and it lasted all night. Giuditta didn't come. I could hear her talking in the next room. She sounded annoyed and in a very bad mood. The next day I was so pale when I got up that papa wanted to send for the doctor. Later, mama called me to her room, and just looking at her face, I felt my knees buckle. She spoke at length about her responsibilities and mine, about my vocation, and the need imposed on me by my poverty to be ruled by that vocation. She spoke of the dangers that a young girl destined for the convent might encounter in the most straightforward relationships, and concluded by telling me that in future, when outsiders came to our house, even the Valentini, I was to stay shut in my room.

My God! how did I endure the torment of those reproofs. She seemed to take delight in needling me, in levelling at me veiled accusations of a thousand misdeeds, and she didn't even make clear to me whether or not she'd discovered that Nino had left the dance to come and find me.

More than once, while she was talking, I felt that I was about to faint, but she didn't notice my pallor, or my trembling, she didn't notice that I had to clutch the back of a chair because I couldn't stand upright any more. If she'd realized the state I was in, she would surely have taken pity on me and spared me this torture. Once I could be alone, I went to bed. My fever had returned. I felt ill, and I wished I were dead.

Giuditta didn't even come then. She was cross with me. My God, what have I done to her? I had the sense of being like one of those criminals that everyone avoids and no one dares to go near ... I felt ashamed before that window, opposite my bed, there, like some adamant accuser. I was hurt by this isolation and neglect. Towards evening I called for my sister – I needed to see her, to be comforted. Even my dear papa looked more serious than usual. Giuditta eventually came, but she seemed very cold. I threw myself into her arms, and I thought the tears that made me feel much better irritated her.

Now I'm alone. Everyone seems to be avoiding me, and I'm hateful to myself. They're right, I'm very much at fault. Only God can pardon me – God whom I've sinned against by loving one of His creatures more than Him.

I sew, I sew, all day long at the window, with the curtains kept scrupulously closed, and I cry when I'm lucky enough not to be seen, and to be able to give vent to my tears. And my eyes sting ... The sky is cloudy, the fields desolate, the rustling of the trees frightens me, the birds don't sing any more ... only occasionally I hear a plaintive nightingale somewhere. Yet I spend hours with my hands crossed in my lap, looking through the window-panes at those huge dark clouds racing westwards, at the treetops slowly swaying and shedding their dead leaves. Winter has arrived in the natural world, just as the winter of the soul has arrived. Carino has flown away, poor thing! I neglected him so much! He's taken his chirpiness and his lively twittering somewhere else, because I'm living in such a gloomy atmosphere. Only Vigilante comes now and again to seek me out, hoping for a smile, expecting me to stroke him. He comes in very quietly, almost hesitantly, questioning me with his beautiful eyes, asking whether he's bothering me. Then he stops in uncertainty, and wags his tail and licks his lips – all of which means to say, 'I'm sorry to be so persistent.' And he comes and lays his head on my lap to tell me that he still loves me, and he looks sad when he goes away, but he still wags his tail and stops at the door to say goodbye.

All day long I can hear the voices of the Valentini talking with my family in another room. Two or three times I've heard a voice that has wrung my heart — his voice.

Him! Him! Always him! Always there's this thorn in my heart, this temptation in my mind, this fever in my blood. Always I see him, before my eyes, there at the window, with his face in his hands. Always in my ears is the sound of his voice, and on my hands the dampness of his tears . . . O God, my God!

Several times I've heard footsteps outside my window, and my heart felt as though it would burst from my breast. I have dizzy spells, faintings fits and bouts of delirium. I can't cry, I can't sleep, I can't pray any more. O Marianna!

What will he think, not seeing me again? Will he know that I've been forbidden to see him? Will he perhaps curse me? Will he be angry? Will he forgive me? You see how far I've fallen? I pray God to make me forget him, and I feel maddened by the mere thought that he might forget me. Sometimes, at dawn, when I'm quite sure that no one might catch me by surprise, I very quietly open the window to look down into the valley, at the house where he lives, where he's probably asleep at that hour, to see his roof, his window, the pot of jasmine, the vine that casts its shade over his door . . . Then I try to guess the spot where he'll rest his elbows on the sill when he opens the window, the clod of earth that he'll first set foot on, his line of vision when he first gazes out, seeking my window . . . for my heart tells me that he will first gaze at my window, and he will know that I was here, watching him sleep, thinking of him, always of him — in my dreams, before I fall asleep, when I first waken, and in my prayers. O Marianna! Pray for this poor sinner who is weaker than her sin. Send me the scapular of Our Lady of Mount Carmel that was blessed in Rome, and send me your little prayer book. I want to think of God. I want to pray to the Virgin, so that she will protect me, and hide me under her mantle of mercy, from the eyes of the world, from myself, my shame and my transgression, and from God's punishment!

I've been ill, my friend, very ill – that's why I haven't written to you. There were days when everyone was crying, and I thanked God for at least granting me the peace of exhaustion. I saw all those pale faces around my bed, all those tears dissimulated with an even more painful smile ... and seeing as though in a dream, my eyes watched calmly. I saw all those dear to me, all of them ... excepting only for him! They must have forbidden him to come. Yet with that exquisite sensitivity of the sick, I sensed he was there, outside the window, crying and praying ... and I kept my eyes that were tired of life fixed on those panes of glasses through which came a ray of winter sunshine that settled on my bed. I couldn't convey to you the feeling I had inside me: I felt calmer, easier, in an atmosphere of peace and serenity; I was still thinking of him, but with such quiet fondness that I felt as if I were among the angels, and one of them, called Nino, had taken me by the hand and called me by name, and as on that night, we'd both looked up at the stars.

It's cloudy, and raining – you know how sad the sound of rain beating against the windowpanes is! Little birds come, shivering, to seek shelter under the eaves, and the wind whistles in the chestnut grove. Apart from this mournful sound, everything is silent. This morning I got out of bed for the first time, tottering and drained of strength. If you could see how I'm writing to you! Supported by a heap of pillows, pausing at every moment to regain energy, to wipe the sweat from my forehead ... and yet it's cold! My head feels heavy, my hand shakes, my thinking's confused and uncertain. They say you came to see me ... I don't remember, Marianna! It must have been one of those days when I was unaware of what was going on around me. This tiny room where I have suffered so much, this trestle-bed, this cruficix, these pieces of furniture seem to have become part of me. I've spent such long hours in a convalescent's state of melancholy inertia, day-dreaming about heaven knows what, gazing at all the objects in my small room, that the shape of the furniture, and, as it were, the cast of the walls, are dear to me. The doctors say that I'm better now, praise God! For the good Lord should always be praised in what He does! My father, Giuditta, Gigi, you and Annetta will all be pleased . . . and he, too!

How sweet it is to return to life after having been on the brink of leaving it — if only to see all these smiling faces, to receive all these signs of affection, to feel loved, to look at the sky, to hear the wind, the rain, the cheeping of the little birds suffering from the cold. Everything looks new and beautiful. It's like the awakening of a tired mind, and its thoughts, turning to something once cherished, with grateful surprise find it even more vital than before. Everything is a source of delight, blessed be God! Everyone takes my pale, thin hand, clasps and kisses it . . . he alone doesn't! he alone!

I got up, swaying and leaning on the furniture, and opened the window. My God! How enchanting is everything I see, even though it's cold, and the ground is covered with snow, and the trees are bare, and the sky is black! I saw that house over there, after such a long time! that vine, that window-sill, that door . . . the jasmine's gone, the vine has lost its leaves, the doors are closed, there's an air of sadness about it all, and yet it seemed like paradise to me . . . I thought I saw the window being closed . . . My God! My eyesight's so weak! I saw a figure behind the shutters . . . It's him, it's him! He saw me! He was waiting for me. O God! O God! Marianna, don't you see? It's him!

At last the doctor's given me permission to step outside in the middle of the day when the weather's fine. They say that I need lots of care because my health's delicate. My poor mother's health was delicate, too, and she died young. Yesterday was Christmas, that wonderful festival that at the convent meant a night of carols and joy, and the moving experience of midnight mass . . . do you remember? The Valentini came every night of the Novena before Christmas to play cards with my family. I heard them talking and laughing in the dining room, where a warm fire had been lit, with doors and windows tightly closed, while the wind moaned outside, and sometimes hail-stones thundered down on the roof. How they must have enjoyed being together, all warm and snug, with the cold and rain outside!

To celebrate the festival we had a special lunch, but without the Valentini . . . because of me, I realized, so that I wouldn't meet him. It was a cheerless occasion compared with the meal we had on my father's name-day, do you remember?

In the morning there was brilliant sunshine. I went and stood outside the door for a while. They wrapped me up in shawls and scarves, and papa supported me. How pleasant and agreeable everything was: a bright sky of the purest azure, the sun gilding the snows that covered Mount Etna, the deep-blue sea, the belltowers of the villages that appeared as white smudges among the trees, the fields with their green grass contrasting with the whiteness of the snow, the wood that was silent because there was no wind and it had no leaves to shed, the lawn on which we'd danced and had such fun, the chickens scratching around in the straw, the little shed that steamed as the snow melted in the sunshine, the birds twittering on the roof, Vigilante stretched out across the threshold, sunning himself, the steward's wife who was hanging out the washing to dry on the bare branches of the chestnut tree, and singing to herself, glancing with ineffable maternal contentment at her two children playing on the doorstep.

Blessed be God! Praise be to God, for the joy and delight He grants to the bird that sings, to the burgeoning leaf, and the basking snake, and the sun that shines, to the mother who holds her baby to her breast, and to my poor soul that rejoices and gives Him thanks.

How early it gets dark in winter! I'd like to have stayed outside for a long time filling my poor tired lungs with that invigorating breeze, and, leaning on my father's arm, to have managed somehow to reach the edge of that lovely chestnut grove where I've spent so many happy hours! I'd like to have sat on that little wall that's covered with green moss. It was cold, the sun was disappearing, down in the valley a thick fog was gathering, and the birds had stopped singing. How mournful the silence of sunset is in winter! My father wanted me to return to the house and go to bed, while the most beautiful moon in the world was glistening on the windowpanes. I wish that at least they'd left me with that lovely moonlight, but they even closed the shutters. I'm ill, you see? It's cold . . . so they had to . . .

They were expecting the Valentini for supper. How wonderful Christmas evening is! Even here, in this solitude, everything has a festive air: the peasant who comes home from the plain, singing, to spend Christmas with his family, the fire crackling beneath a big cauldron, the village girls who dance to the sound of bagpipes. I saw the preparations going on in the kitchen for the meal, the wood in the grate, the candles and playing cards left ready on the table, and a plate of sweets and a few bottles of liqueur set out on the desk by the window – all the pleasant trappings of a homely Christmas evening. I counted the chairs placed around the table – there were eight . . . mine wasn't there any more . . . I saw the place where I used to sit and the chair that he took beside me when he looked at my cards.

I thought about all these things as I lay in bed, all alone, in that tiny little room which is dark, silent and gloomy-looking. I would like to have fallen asleep, and not to have heard the talking, those voices, that festiveness close by . . . I spent an extremely restless night, without a wink of sleep. I think I've still got a fever. I feel so weak! I held my breath all evening trying to hear what he said and to tell from the sound of his voice whether he was sad or happy. I heard him three times: once he said, 'thank you', then 'it's my turn', and the last time, 'signorina'. If you could only imagine all that these words convey! If I could only express it!

They played until midnight. I could hear them from here. Then they sat down to eat . . . Now I'm tired, my head is swimming . . . I wrote to you to keep myself awake . . . to give myself something to do . . .

Let's talk about you instead . . . Did you have a good Christmas? Are you happy and cheerful?

I want to amaze myself; I want to regain my strength in the next few days; I want to overcome this terrible affliction. God who is merciful will help me! Write to me, write to me! Perhaps we'll see each other soon, and we'll have so much to tell each other!

Oh, Marianna! My dear Marianna! How I've cried! How I've suffered! The Valentini are leaving tomorrow, do you realize? There's no cholera any more, there's nothing! They're leaving . . .

I shan't see him again. I found out by accident, a few moments ago. They didn't even have the grace to tell me . . .

I thought I'd die. I regretted that God had ever made me get better. I cried the whole night. My chest hurts a lot. I sometimes sobbed so loudly that Giuditta must have heard.

I'm completely shameless! I've no restraint any more. I've only one thought. I went out like a madwoman to ask the steward's wife for information. It's tomorrow! He came to say goodbye to my family, and they didn't even let me see him for the last time! And I shan't ever see him again . . . and it was after nightfall when I found out, when it was already dark . . . when I couldn't see any more to look at the little house where he'll be spending his last night!

My God! what kind of people are these . . . that are so heartless, without pity or tears?

What a night, what a horrible night! How cramped this little room is, and how miserable it is here! All night long the rain beat against the window-panes, the wind rattled the shutters, the thunder sounded as if it would bring the roof of the house down on us, and the sinister flashes of lightning were discernible even from inside . . . I was afraid and dared not cross myself . . . I'm damned, excommunicated, for even at that moment I thought only of him . . . more than once I prayed to God, hoping that this storm would last, I don't know how long, provided he didn't leave, that he remained always near by me . . . That's all – not to see him, not to speak to him, but to know that he was there, down in the valley, beneath that roof, behind that window, so that I could send him my greetings in the morning, and with my eyes embrace that threshold, that earth, that air . . . Is that too much to ask? My God! If I can be content with that . . .

But hasn't he realized that I'm pining away for him? That I'm weak and ill? Hasn't he cried? Hasn't he suffered as well? Why hasn't he come, for a moment, one single moment, just for one last sight of him, to say goodbye to me from afar?

Why hasn't he let me hear the sound of his voice? Why hasn't he been through the wood? Why hasn't he fired his gun into the air? Why hasn't he got his dog to bark – the dog that he asked me if I loved, on whose head he placed his hand next to mine . . .

O God! O God!

I'm writing to you in bed, with a big book resting on my knees. Sometimes I shiver with cold, and I'm overcome with dizziness, but if I didn't write to you I couldn't stand being shut up in here – I think I'd go mad. I've no tears left, and anguish devours me like a rabid dog. I feel frenzied, feverish, and delirious. This falling rain and whistling wind, these claps of thunder and flashes of lightning are unbearable. This roof presses down on me, these walls suffocate me. I wish I could open the window, and feel that icy rain beating on my forehead, and drink in that cold wind. I wish I could enjoy the lightning, the storm that howls and writhes and moans like me. If I'd only known that I'd have to suffer so much . . . Why did these merciless people take me away from the convent? Why didn't they leave me there to die, alone, and helpless, of cholera and neglect?

Hush! Listen, Marianna! Didn't you hear? I thought . . . there, at the window, amid the tumult of wind and rain . . . a footstep . . . Yes, yes, it's him . . . it's him!

My heart's bursting, and I'm clutching my head with both hands, because it feels as though I'm also losing my mind . . . It's him! What's he doing? What does he want? He's knocking at the window! O God! Let me die, let me die! He's saying goodbye ... and I... my God, what's happening inside me ...

I've had a coughing fit ... that's my farewell ... He must have heard. I can't see any more ... I feel terrible ... My God! What if they were to find me with this shameful letter?

God had mercy on me: I opened my eyes and found this letter still in my hands. No one saw it. The door's still closed. The sunlight's already entering my room through all the vents in the shutters. The birds are twittering on the sill. The sun! How horrible it is! But what about the storm? And what about . . .

I leap out of bed . . . I haven't the strength to stand upright . . . I haven't the courage to open the window . . . And yet . . .

My God, thy will be done!

It's all over! I saw that silent house, the shutters closed, and over the entire surroundings an air of heart-breaking quietness, desolation and abandonment.

I consulted the sky that saw us as neighbours, the trees that rustled over his head, the mountains we still shared a few hours ago, that are now lonely, sad, and forsaken . . .

He's gone, he's gone!

Under my window, in ground made soft by the rain and white with snow, I saw his footprints . . . his last footprints! He stood there, and his hand touched the sill . . . he was here! Here! This air surrounded him, and everything that I see, he saw . . . And now he's gone and there's nothing left! Nothing!

I found a withered rose lying on the window-sill, a poor rose that he'd more or less stolen from me, and that I had let him steal. The rain has ruined it. It's a memento. I have it here on my breast . . . and when I'm shorn, I'll lay this poor dead flower on my hair and send it to my sister . . .

Today is our last day at Monte Ilice. Tomorrow morning we leave for Catania. If we pass through Mascalucia, I shall see you.

If you could only see how miserable everything is here! The cloudy sky, the chilly atmosphere, the valleys shrouded in mist and the mountains covered with snow, the trees that have lost their leaves and the birds that have lost their cheerfulness, the pallid sun, the long black lines of crows wheeling through the air, cawing, and the country folk huddled round their fires.

My family can't stay on here any longer, by themselves, in the cold weather, and now that the fear of cholera's past, papa can't wait to leave. I spend hours thinking, of heaven knows what, leaning on my sill when it's sunny, or gazing sorrowfully at the sky through the window-panes.

My God! This is death . . . the death of nature, and of the heart . . . and of that poor rose . . .

And to think how beautiful this place was! And how happy I was here!

I'm reconciled with God and with my vocation. I've realized that peace, calm and tranquillity are only to be found there, in that cell, at the foot of that cross. And that all worldly pleasures – every single one of them! – leave you with a sense of bitterness in the end.

Yet I feel that I'm leaving a bit of my heart in this place where I've spent so many hours of sadness and so many days of joy. At the sight of every object, I thought, 'After tomorrow, I shan't ever see that again!' This evening I went for a last walk in the woods. I sat for the last time on the wall. I gazed at the little cottage opposite our front door, and standing at the window I contemplated with an inexplicable sense of sorrow the trees, the mountains with their ravines, and the sky from which daylight was fading . . . and I took final leave of them, and even of the moss-covered stone and of the eaves over my head. All these things have a special look, the melancholy look of things that seem to say farewell ... And mine is an eternal farewell. In the coming year, when these mountains that now stand silent and dreary are alive with sounds and smells and brightness, when the village girls sing in the vineyards and the lark up in the skies, my family will return ... They'll see these lovely places again ... but not I! I'll be far away, enclosed in the convent ... for ever.

I gazed at his house again ... it looks sad and frightened, alone, cold and silent, lost at the bottom of the valley. I closed my window for the last time. I watched as the twilight faded from these window-panes and the stars came out in the firmament, one by one. By the light of the last evening's candle the walls have a special look: this trestle-bed, this crucifix, these pieces of furniture, all these little things have become animate, they're sad, and they've wished me goodbye ... And I am sad ... I cried, and my heart felt lighter.

My dear Marianna, if you were expecting to see me, there was no point – we didn't go through Mascalucia; it would have made our journey much longer and the weather was bad. We've been here since yesterday evening, and tomorrow I'm going back to the convent . . .

We left Monte Ilice at about ten, with rain threatening, but that couldn't be helped – everything was ready for our departure and mama wouldn't have wanted to unpack the trunks and cases again, not for all the gold in the world. And so much the better – what was the point of staying there any longer? Even the sky seemed to be driving us away. Nevertheless, I crossed the threshold of that house with a heavy heart.

I wanted to take a last look at those little rooms, the lawn, the steward's cottage, the dry-stone wall, that fine chestnut tree with its branches spread over the roof. I fondly touched the walls and the furniture in my little room. I opened my window for the last time, to hear the hinges creak. I walked round the house to see my window from the outside, as he must have seen it . . . to try to identify the place where he stood . . .

Everyone was happy – Giuditta, Gigi, papa and mama. Vigilante frisked about, poor thing, not realizing that we were deserting him. The steward's wife wished us a safe journey, while her children clung to her skirts. A little bird shivering with cold came and settled on a small leafless branch of the tree, and it, too, began to cheep plaintively.

We set off on foot. The mules were waiting at the bottom of the valley to take us down to Trecastagne, for as you know, you can't come up these mountains any more except on horseback. Every now and again, we'd turn to take a last look at the place we were leaving. At the bend in the lane, further down in the valley, we passed by his house . . . I didn't have the heart to look, and yet the smallest details are engraved on my mind. His window has green shutters and one of the panes of glass is broken. On the sill there's a patch of damp where the pot of jasmine used to be. The wind has ripped away the vine from above the door, and cast it to the ground. On the lawn in front of the door lie bits of broken glass and scraps of letters and rain-sodden newspapers blown this way and that by the wind, and there's still a broken pipe on the sill. All these things speak, and what they say is, 'He's not here any more! He's gone away! We're alone!'

This was the lane that he took to come to us. He must have walked along it so often! From there, he'd have seen our house peeping through the chestnut trees – countless times he must have seen it! And countless times he must have rested his gaze on these moss-covered stones, and sat here with his splendid dog lying at his feet . . . Marianna, I can't bear all these memories!

The mules took us down to Trecastagne, where the carriage was waiting for us. Poor Vigilante was all over us, urging us to take him along. What could I do? I gave him a hug, and it almost brought tears to my eyes to see him being forcibly dragged away by the steward, who put him on a leash.

I turned to take a last look at my beloved Monte Ilice. I could no longer see the house, the cottage, or the vineyard, only the brown mass of the forest; the rest was lost in the mist, and white with snow. We climbed into the carriage and left.

When we came into town, my heart lightened immensely. I looked out of the window and seemed to recognize him in every person I encountered . . . They must have thought me shameless! When I saw a group of people, I couldn't help sticking my head out of the window – I was all in a turmoil, sure that I was going to see him there . . . The carriage went swiftly past, and it wrung my heart to think that I hadn't time to pick him out among those people. Does anyone know where the Valentini live? This question came to my lips countless times, but I didn't have the courage to voice it. Catania's so vast! It's not like being in our beloved mountains, where you always knew where to find someone you were looking for. These great roads seemed forbidding, all these people looked sad. We arrived at the house – my stepmother's house . . . I felt like a stranger in the family . . . they were all so delighted to be back . . .

I wonder whether the Valentini will be aware of our arrival, and whether they'll come? I wonder whether I'll see him passing in the street? O God! Our street's so deserted! No one comes here for a walk . . . unless . . . But he might . . . Who knows where he could be walking at this moment? And what if I were seen at the window?

My stepmother's told me that I'm going back to the convent tomorrow. She must have thought this would comfort me – she doesn't realize that I felt chilled with terror . . .

I'd stopped thinking about it . . . But I must resign myself . . . That's my home. God will forgive me and soothe this poor heart that should never have gone away from Him.

I shall see my cell again, my crucifix, my flowers, the church, my fellow postulants . . . all except you! You're not coming back to the convent! The Lord's will be done. At least you'll occasionally come to visit your poor friend who's so unhappy . . . Who knows whether I'll be able to write to you and confide in you any more?

Goodbye! Goodbye!

These few lines are perhaps the last that I shall write to you. The carriage is waiting below. Papa, mama, Gigi and Giuditta are all dressed up to accompany me.

I've cried. I'm now wiping my eyes and taking my last breath of freedom.

The Valentini came to say goodbye. He wasn't with them. They hugged me. How Annetta and I cried!

I shall go downstairs and climb into the carriage, and in twenty minutes it will all be over.

Goodbye to you, too, goodbye. My heart is breaking.

I didn't want to let the end of the month go by without writing to you. You might have thought that I was sad and unhappy, whereas here, at the foot of the altar, in the austere observance of our rule, I've found, if not peace, at least a quietness of heart.

It's true, that you get a feeling of overwhelming dismay as you enter this place, and hear the door shut behind you, suddenly seeing yourself bereft of air and light, down in these corridors, amid this tomb-like silence and monotonous drone of prayer. Everything saddens the heart and instills it with fear: those black figures to be seen passing beneath the dim light of the lamp burning before the crucifix, figures that meet without speaking to each other, and walk without a sound, as if they were ghosts; the flowers withering in the garden; the sun that tries in vain to penetrate the opaque glass in the windows; the iron railings; and the brown twill curtains. You can hear the world going on outside, its sounds faded to a whisper, deadened by these walls. Everything that comes from outside is weak and muted. I'm alone among one hundred other forsaken souls.

I've also lost the consolation of my family. I can only see them in the presence of lots of other people, in a big gloomy room, through the double grating over the window. We can't hold hands. All homely intimacy is gone, leaving nothing but phantoms speaking to each other through the screens, and I'm always wondering if that really is my father, the father who used to smile at me and hug me; if that's the same Giuditta who used to dance with me; and if that's the Gigi who used to be so bright and cheerful. Now, they're grave, cold and melancholy. They look at me through the grille, as if peering into a tomb, in which they, the living, observe corpses that talk and move.

Yet all these hardships, all these austere practices serve to detach the heart from earthly frailty, isolating it, making it think of itself, and imparting to it the still calm that comes from God and from the thought that our pilgrimage on earth is thereby shortened. I've confessed. I confessed everything – everything! That kindly priest took pity on my poor sick heart. He comforted and counselled me, and helped me to tear the demon from my breast. I feel freer, easier, more worthy of God's mercy.

Tomorrow I begin my noviciate. They tried to delay it for a few more days because of my delicate health (I've never completely recovered from the illness I suffered up at Monte Ilice: I have a fever every two or three days, and every night I cough), but God will give me the strength to endure the ordeal of this noviciate. From now on, only very rarely will we be able to see each other, and I won't be able to write to you because I shan't so often see Filomena, the kind-hearted lay sister who has been sending you my letters.

I shan't even be seeing my poor papa any more . . . The Lord's will be done!

Marianna, pray for me to God, that I might undergo this trial with resignation.

I've completed my noviciate. I was granted a dispensation because of my health, which is still very poor. I often have a fever, I cough, and I've grown so weak that the least effort exhausts me. Yet my heart is at peace, and that is the greatest blessing God could have granted me. Sometimes frailty rebels, and temptation assails me again. Then I prostrate myself at the foot of the altar, I spend all night kneeling on the cold paving of the chancel, I mortify my body with fasting and penance, and when the flesh is subdued and passions quelled, temptation is overcome and peace returns.

This year of trial has been very difficult, but God has enabled me to triumph. I saw my family depart at the sudden outbreak of cholera last summer, and I felt abandoned even by my loved ones ... I went out on the terrace and fixed my gaze on that wonderful place where I was with them for a while ... Ah, what good times they were! I thought of many things ... yes, admittedly, I cried, and sometimes I felt weak, but in the end I triumphed.

Everything here serves to close the mind in on itself, to circumscribe it, to render it mute, blind and deaf to all that is not God. Yet even at the foot of the cruficix, when those temptations assailed me, and I remembered our little house, those fields, the cottage, the fire on which the steward's wife used to cook her soup, I'd think about that poor peasant-woman, cuddling her babies on her lap, without any of my temptations, doubts and regrets, and I wondered whether she might not be closer to God than I who mortify my rebellious spirit with many penances.

How often have I not envisaged those mountains, woods and bright sky! And how often have I not said, 'At this time of day, they're sitting together beneath the chestnut tree. Now, they're strolling down the paths through the vineyard, and now Vigilante is barking, and the birds are twittering under the eaves! And when I've awakened as if from a dream, I've found my face all wet with tears.

And then there's another thought ... another ghost ... there ... always there, fixed before my eyes ... at the foot of the cross, in the midst of the crowd attending mass, at my bedside, behind that green twill curtain – the temptation that grabs me by the hair, and drags me from my prayer, that makes me cry and sends me into a frenzy ...

There have been times when I thought I was going mad – and I thanked God for it, because the mad are blameless. I think I see him down among all those people in the church, on Sundays. I cross myself, and appalled, in tears, I rush to the foot of my confessor. The good old man tries to comfort me, and he prescribes the penances supposed to remove this stain from my heart but that prove ineffectual because I'm a great sinner ...

Yet he might have come to church at least once ... to hear mass ... without even looking up at the choir ... but only to show himself ... He must know that I'm here, and he hasn't tried to see me!

O God! Forgive me, Marianna ... you see how much at fault and how wretched I am! It's the devil assailing me when I least expect it ... How often, when praying to the Lord to take this cross away from me, have I not looked down into the church to see if he were there, searching for him among the crowd! And my prayer has died on my lips! And my thoughts have lingered on him ... lost in reverie, dreaming of running through the fields, of listening for his footstep and that knock on the window, gazing up at those stars, touching that hand as it stroked that fine gun-dog's head, and hearing in my ears the name 'Maria', that might have come from heaven ...

O God! I'm weak and very frail ... but I fight and struggle with myself ... My God, I'm not to blame! It's stronger than me, stronger than my will, my remorse and my faith.

You write that you are happy, and glad to be outside the convent. My dear Marianna, thank the good Lord for sparing your mother, and for sparing you from being born poor, for not having driven this thorn into your heart, or having made you weak, hysterical, excitable and sickly.

Only when this flesh is dissolved will I cease to suffer. That's why I would like to detach myself from the world that clings to me stubbornly, and I look up to heaven and raise my arms in entreaty . . .

Now that I've been reunited with my dear Filomena, who takes pity on my sorrows and allows me the comfort of writing to you and receiving your letters, I'll write to you a few more times before taking my solemn vows. You will come to the ceremony, won't you?

I want to say goodbye, through the grille, amid the clouds of incense and the sound of the organ, to all those who are dear to me. I want all those friendly faces to sustain me in this difficult step, because my poor heart is frail. I need to be able to gaze into your eyes, and those of my papa, my sister, Gigi, and Annetta, when I hear the rasp of the scissors in my hair . . .

I'm scared, Marianna, I'm scared! I'm scared of those scissors . . . of that moment . . . I'm scared of him . . . if he were to come to the church that day . . . My God! No, no, I'm weak . . . for pity's sake . . . You'll come with my father, Giuditta, my brother, mama, Annetta and the Valentini . . . My God! Thy will be done!

My dear Marianna, my sister . . . I thought I was inured to pain, but this has caught me unawares, rending me, crushing me, annihilating me! Here I am, weaker and more wretched than before! My God! And now this! Now this!

Do you know what I've heard, Marianna? Do you know what I've heard? Could you ever have imagined it! I've been extremely ill for more than two weeks. Now I'm up, writing to share my tears with you.

What is this wretched thing inside me that groans and suffers, that can't tear itself away from all this misery and raise itself to God?

They shouldn't have told me . . .They've no mercy! No, it's just I'm weak. It's my fault, and God is punishing me.

Signor Nino is going to marry my sister . . . do you hear? They came to bring me the glad tidings! It's a good marriage . . . they're both rich . . . Giuditta is pleased and happy . . . I didn't have the courage to ask them to spare me the ordeal of the usual visit . . . because he will come, too . . . I sense that I shan't have the strength for this further sacrifice . . . it will kill me . . .

And will he have the strength for it?

Yet I'll pray so hard to God . . . for me . . . and for him . . . I'll flagellate myself and weep so much that God will give both of us the strength to get through this cruel ordeal.

I've cried until I've no tears left to shed.

My chest aches, my mind is wandering. I wish I could sleep. Most of all, I wish the Lord would spare me this pain . . .

God's will be done!

28 February, midnight

Praise be to God! The ordeal's over. I thought I'd die, but it's in the past now, all over and done with ...

They'd informed me, as well as all the other nuns in our family, the abbess and the novice mistress. We waited in the big hall outside the parlour. I was sitting between Mother Superior and the novice mistress. They arrived exactly on time. I heard the carriage stop at the door, and the sound of their footsteps as they climbed the stairs and approached the grille. I rose unsteadily to my feet ... I couldn't see anything ... I heard the bell summoning me ... The novice mistress opened the curtain. I clung to the drapes and collapsed on to the wooden bench. I saw a blur of faces crowding the grille, but they couldn't have seen me – it was dark on this side. They talked. After a while I was able to hear them. My stepmother talked, and so did papa ... Giuditta didn't say anything, and neither did he ... My sister, wearing a pink dress and matching bonnet, looked happy. He was sitting beside her, holding his hat, and stroking it with his gloves. I didn't cry ... It seemed as though I was dreaming. I was surprised not to be suffering more ... Then they stood up. My father said goodbye to me, mama gave me a smile,. Giuditta blew me a kiss, Gigi asked for some sweets ... He bowed. I watched him walk away. He was at Giuditta's side. At the door he gave her his arm. Then the door closed, their footsteps faded away until they couldn't be heard any more. The carriage left ... and silence remained. Nothing else! Nothing! I'm alone!

In a month's time I shall take the veil. Preparations for the occasion are already under way. Everyone showers me with affection. Not a day goes by that papa and mama don't come to see me. They want to celebrate the event. There'll be music, fireworks, and guests. My dear papa seems happy that I, too, should be gaining status, as he puts it. Giuditta has also come, several times. If you could only see how beautiful her happiness makes her! God bless her!

And you, too, are engaged to be married, my dear Marianna. You write that you're happy. I hope so. But in your happiness don't forget your poor friend who has more need than ever of your affection. Come and see me once in a while, when you have time. If you only knew how happy I am in those few rare moments when I see the people who love me. You know, it's an act of charity to visit poor prisoners!

You who are betrothed, you who are happy, tell me what joy and celebration and jubilation my sister must be feeling. Tell me what must be in her heart at the prospect of remaining for ever at her beloved's side, free of doubt, remorse and fear, blessed and feted and cosseted by everyone. Tell me what happiness it must be to think that she will be his, and that he will belong to her; that she will see him every day, at every hour, and hear him speak; that she will rest on his arm, and whisper in his ear everything that passes through her mind; that she will be called by his name, and see the day when she will cradle his children in her arms and teach them to love him, and to pray for him to the good Lord. To think that everything will be a joy, and there will be no end to that joy. How good the Lord is, to grant such happiness! I've been told that the wedding's on Sunday . . . God bless them!

Sunday, 29 March, midnight

My dear Marianna, I'm writing to you from my cell, by night, afraid that my small light might be seen through the curtain and even this meagre comfort of being completely open-hearted with you will be taken away from me. What a day this has been for me, Marianna! Will my suffering never end?

I'm alone, shivering with cold. All is silence. There's only the sound of the clock's pendulum, like the footsteps of a ghost moving down these long, dark corridors. I spent all day in the chancel, praying and weeping before God. Now I'm weak and tired, I can't take any more, but I'm a little calmer. Today's Sunday! You'll appreciate the full significance of that word – I'll say no more ... It was today!

You know, they brought me refreshments from the wedding! Don't they remember I'm ill and that such things would be bad for me?

Yet how were they to remember? Everyone's so happy, this is a day of rejoicing ... It's my fault for being such a poor sickly, tiresome wretch. What a celebration it must have been!

I couldn't sleep at all last night. And they can't have slept either, waiting for this Sunday to dawn ... dreaming, open-eyed, of those flowers and wedding outfits, of the crowd and those smiling faces ...

I, too, pictured all those things. I saw Giuditta, looking so beautiful in her bridal gown, with her white veil and crown of orange blossom, and him, holding out his hand, smiling at her ... They entered the church, surrounded by friends and relatives, by their loved ones ... The altar was all lit up, and the organ was playing. Then they knelt down and called on God as a witness to their happiness.

God who is merciful must have allowed him to forget that evening when he took my hand, and the words that he said to me, and the starlight, and that stormy night

113

when he came to say goodbye to me, and his knock at the window, and my coughing fit . . .

I, too, have forgotten . . . I want to forget . . .

It's all over now . . . everything . . .

You see, Marianna, that I'm resigned, that God has taken pity on me! Tomorrow I'll be preparing myself for this great step with spiritual exercises. I shan't write to you; I shan't see anybody ever again, not even my father. This is a torment to me.

Could that happy couple, in the tumult of their happiness, have spared a few moments' thought for this poor woman, dying here, alone and forsaken?

Come to the ceremony. It'll be on Sunday, 6 April – another Sunday, as you see . . . only this will be a sad one! Will you come? I'll expect you. Goodbye (don't you think this is a very gloomy word?).

I'm writing a hurried note to remind you that I'm expecting you, that I have need of you, all of you, that I have need of strength and courage.

They brought me my veil, flowers and new gown – it's a lovely bridal gown. The final preparations are being made. Tomorrow's the day . . .

You should see what unusual activity there is, what excitement and jubilation! It's a festive occasion for all these poor recluses. This vast sepulchre only comes to life when it opens up for another victim.

It's a lovely April day. The weather has been bad until today, but now there's brilliant sunshine. I went out on the terrace for a last breath of life.

I saw so many things from up there, Marianna – the fields, the sea, that huge mass of buildings, and Etna, far away in the distance . . . And all these things seemed to have an air of sadness about them . . .

I'd like to have seen Monte Ilice one last time, and our little house, and that lovely chestnut grove . . . I couldn't, nor shall I ever see them again . . . I feel a pang, here, in my heart!

A hubbub from the road reaches the belvedere – the sound of carts and carriages, of voices, of people working, to-ing and fro-ing . . . All these people going about their business have their joys and sorrows, they work, and live . . . And these birds fly far away from here . . .

Tomorrow, in a few hours' time, between me and all this life around me will rise an insurmountable wall, an abyss, a word, a vow . . .

How shall I get through this coming night? If only I had you here with me, at least . . .

I'm scared!

God, sustain me!

My sister! Have you ever heard the dead speak from the grave?

I'm dead! Your poor Maria is dead. They laid me out on the bier and covered me with a funeral shroud, they recited the requiem, and the bells tolled . . . It's as though something funereal were weighing on my spirit and my limbs were inert. Between me and the world – nature, life – there's something heavier than a tombstone, more silent than the grave.

It's a terrifying spectacle – that of Death amid the exuberance of life and the tumult of the passions, that of the soul seen by the body to expire, of matter surviving spirit.

I open my eyes as though in a trance. I gaze out into infinity, amid this darkness, and silence, this still calm . . . Everything is infinitely distant. I see you as in a dream, beyond the confines of reality. Is it you that has vanished into the void, or I that have strayed into nothingness?

I'm still in a daze. I feel as though I were wandering about in a vast tomb, as though all this were a dream . . . that it couldn't last for ever, and I was bound to wake up. I witnessed a solemn spectacle, but it didn't seem to be for me . . . I felt that I, like everyone else, was attending a funeral, a lugubrious religious ceremony, but that when the music fell silent and all the bells stopped ringing, when the candles were extinguished and the priests filed out to the sacristy, when all those people got up to leave, I, too, would leave and not have to remain alone here . . . where I feel scared . . . I saw all that funereal, heart- wringing ceremonial – and was I at the centre of it all? Was I the one that was dying? Those people in their Sunday best, that music and bell-ringing, those lights – were they all for me? And could I possibly have consented to die? Could I have been willing to die?

They dressed me as a bride, with a veil, a crown, and

flowers. They told me I was beautiful. God forgive me, but I was pleased, only because he would have seen me like that! They led me up to the grille. You saw me. I couldn't see anybody – I saw a cloud of incense, a blurred throng, and many candles burning, and I heard the organ playing. Then they closed the curtain, stripped me of that lovely gown, removed the veil and flowers, and clothed me in a habit, without my having any awareness of what was happening. I couldn't see or hear anything . . . I let them do as they pleased, but I was trembling so much that my teeth were chattering. I thought of my sister's lovely wedding dress, of the ceremony she would have taken part in without experiencing the dismay that then overwhelmed me. The curtain was drawn back again. All the people were still there, watching, listening, with an avid curiosity that chilled me with inexplicable terror. They loosened my hair and I felt it come right down over my hands, which I kept joined together. They gathered it all up in a fistful . . . then came a rasp of steel . . . I thought I'd been seized with a shiver of fever, but it was the touch of coolness on my neck from that cold implement in my hair. Otherwise, I had only a confused idea of what was happening. I saw my father, crying. Why was he crying? I saw my mother, Giuditta, and Gigi . . . At Giuditta's side there was another person looking very pale, and watching me with staring eyes. At that moment the rasp of those cold scissors seemed to drown the priests' chanting, the organ music, and my father's sobs. My hair fell all around me in heaps of curls, in whole tresses . . . and tears fell from my eyes. Then the organ became mournful, and it sounded to me as though the bells were lamenting. They laid me on the bier, and covered me with a funeral pall. All those black figures gathered round me; pale and as impassive as ghosts, they watched me, chanting, with candles in their hands. The curtain closed. From the church came the shuffling of all those people leaving. Everyone was abandoning me, even my father. The ghosts hugged me, and kissed me. They had cold lips and they smiled without making a sound.

All this meant that I was dying! And how was it that it took only this to quieten all the passions seething in my breast? To stifle them? How could that ceremony – the candles, the bier, the scissors – have had the power to leave me devoid of feeling, and my senses dulled. How had they got me to bury myself alive, and give up all God's blessings – air, light, freedom, and love?

And still I'm sinning! Still! Even after I'm dead! But my sin will die, too. Here, where my heart used to be, there's nothing now. These are the last throes of life, the struggle of a spirit that doesn't want to die. I think, I groan, I'm troubled and distressed, but it won't be for long. I spent the whole night unable to sleep, or dream, or think. What have they done to me? What have they done? That's what I ask myself in terror. All night, that face is always there, above the curtain ... his face ... that watched me, pale and silent, with staring eyes, while the scissors rasped incessantly in my hair. I haven't the strength to cry any more: I'm overwhelmed with emptiness.

No, it's not true! The strange mystery that has taken place hasn't brought me any closer to God. It's left me in the dark, in the void; it's annihilated me. I don't know what's inside me any more: there's a silence that terrifies me.

I'm writing to you from my bed. I'm very ill. My dear Marianna, if you could only see how the fever has devoured my flesh. I look at my poor pale and trembling hands, and they're so thin that I think I can see the blood flowing through my veins. I have a hot, burning sensation here in my chest.

Today I'm feeling a little better, and I'm strong enough to write to you. I wish I could chat to you and think of those happy days that were full of life and joy, but everything around me is so dismal that even if I close my eyes and dream of the past, I don't have the heart to smile. I've been very poorly, but the Lord hasn't forsaken me. They've transferred me to the sick-room, which was a great blow. At least in my little cell I had lots of memories that, although painful, I nevertheless cherished; but here, everything seems so gloomy, as if every sick nun had left behind the spectre of her suffering. Who knows how many nuns have died here? Perhaps in this very bed! And as these thoughts occur to me, during the long, sleepless nights when I'm racked with fever, I'm seized with an uncontrollable shudder, and I see ghosts shrouded in black veils creeping quietly along the walls, causing the dim light of the lamp in the corridor to waver . . . and I feel scared and hide my head under the sheets. I cry from morning until evening, remembering that dear little room at Monte Ilice with its friendly walls that knew me, where I was with my family, with that lovely sunshine and fresh air, and those beloved faces . . . And when my heart has more need of comfort and affection, all I see around me are the faces of the nursing sisters, grown impassive through familiarity with the sight of suffering. And the light that comes through the window is pale, wan, and sickly. Joyful spring has visited the earth without sending a single one of its festive colours to this forsaken corner of pain and misery.

Yesterday a little white butterfly came flitting by and

settled on the window-pane. You, who've been blessed by God, and are able to see the sun and fill your lungs with deep breaths of fresh air, can't conceive of the sense of tenderness a butterfly's visit, or the scent of a flower can bring to the heart of a sick nun! It's as though the whole joyful panoply of spring – the perfumed breeze, the greenness of the meadows, the skylark's early-morning song – were gathered round that butterfly and had come to cheer the sad home of all these desolate women. Alas, having rested for a moment on that sorry little flower growing out of a crack in the window-sill, the butterfly flew off, fluttering its wings, and disappeared into the blue. It was free, and happy, and perhaps had seen all these pale faces and all these tears!

In two or three days, I hope to be able to get up for an hour or two. I'll force myself, as long as they let me return to my little cell . . . as long as they let me out of here . . .

Who knows when I'll be able to see you again? I feel so drained of strength that it seems to me that I may never get out of this bed again.

I've come back to this letter two or three times, and yet you couldn't possibly imagine how much effort it's cost me to write it . . . However, it's been a great comfort . . . the only comfort left to me. I wish I could keep on chatting to you, because in the meantime I stop thinking about my suffering, about being here . . . and lots of other horrible things besides. But now I'm exhausted. I've written a long letter, haven't I – a very long letter for a poor sick person like me! You'll have some difficulty in deciphering my writing because my hand's unsteady, but you love me, so you'll be able to tell what I've written . . . and what I haven't written.

I should thank God even for this illness. It's somewhat stupefying. I feel as though I'm dreaming, and I still don't fully understand what's happened to me . . . When I wake up, God will give me strength . . .

Goodbye.

Why have you all abandoned me, Marianna? Even my father! Even you! Here I am, all alone, suffering, in this huge corridor, where there's not a ray of sunshine, and no loving faces. I'm in a state that would wring compassion from a stone. I'm going to die, Marianna. Your poor friend will die here and never see you, or her father, again.

I thought I was getting better; I'd hoped to be leaving this dreadful sick-room. I've got worse, and no one's hiding from me the seriousness of my condition.

If I were to die here, alone!

The nights are terrible, Marianna! Those long hours that never end! That flickering light, that crucifix, those gloomy pictures, those stifled groans, that snoring from the nursing sisters asleep in the armchairs. I have a raging thirst and daren't disturb the sisters, who grumble, poor things, when they keep being wakened. Last night I tried to drag myself over to the little table to quench the burning dryness inside me. I felt as if I were going mad with thirst. But I'd no sooner got out of bed than I fell to the ground in a faint, and cut my head badly. I was found in a pool of blood . . .

Dawn comes, pale, sad, and unsmiling. Night falls, full of fears and shadows. I think of my father, my little family, of all those things that would allay even these present sufferings, and I cry and cry, and my chest feels sore.

My God! If I were to die here? If I were to die . . . without seeing my father?

It must be a terrible moment, Marianna! I'm frightened at the thought of being alone, with no one to comfort me . . . If I could only see my father, at least! Don't you think it's barbarous not to let us see those dearest to us at least one last time at that solemn moment? The only comfort I have is that of writing to them, as I write to you. But when I can't write any more – what then? If my papa had any knowledge of even a fraction of what I'm suffering!

It costs me so much effort to write to you. In those rare moments when I feel a little revived, I force myself to write two or three lines: it makes me feel that I have a hold on life again – and I assure you that I cling to it desperately. But my hand shakes so much that I can't even read what I've written, and I'm so feeble-headed I don't know what my mind is telling me. I have to come back to the letter ten times to write ten lines.

That charitable soul Filomena comes to see me every day and brings me your news. God bless her for the comfort she gives to this poor sick woman! I can't tell you how precious to my desolate heart is the smallest favour, or the least sign of sympathy ... I've such great need of being loved ... and loving intensely, since life is slipping away from me!

O Marianna! Tomorrow they're going to give me the Last Rites! Is my condition so serious, then?

Yet I don't feel as if I'm about to die . . .

O God, thy will be done!

Outside the window the sun's still shining, and you can hear the sound of all those people moving about, living . . . a sunbeam coming through the window has settled on my bed . . .

What a world there is in a ray of sunshine! Everything it sees and casts its light on at any moment . . . countless joys, and sorrows, and people who love each other . . . and him!

Under the eaves there's a swallow's nest – the sun shines for them, too . . .

O God!

Yet how can I die without seeing my father? May I never see him again? O God! I'm resigned to dying, but I wish I could see my father one last time . . . Poor papa, who doesn't know that I'm dying . . . Why haven't they told him? Why haven't they sent for him? There's no telling how much he'll grieve for me!

To think of dying – of dying so young . . . I'm not yet twenty!

O God!

When will I die? If I could at least die quickly! This spiritual torment is so painful!

I've made my confession. How terrifying, Marianna, how terrifying!

While everything going on around me was speaking to me of the next life, I was still thinking of him! And with all the nuns kneeling around me, reciting litanies, his name was on my lips!

What a gloomy ceremony, with those candles, that bell, that canopy, that chanting!

Goodbye to all those I love, to my father, Marianna, my sister, Gigi . . . and to you . . . goodbye.

O Marianna, tell him that I was thinking of him even at this moment!

O Marianna! Marianna! Thank the Lord! I'm not dead . . .
I may well live . . . God will show me His mercy, and let
me see my dear ones again . . .

They've told me that even this hope is a sin, and that we
must resign ourselves to the will of God . . . Lord, forgive
me for this desire, but my heart is weak and feeble . . .

O God is merciful! I shan't die! The doctor says that I'm getting better . . .

I'm going to live, Marianna, I'm going to live! God's letting me live! I'm so weak . . . I pray . . . I bless the Lord . . . and when I see that sunbeam glistening on the window-pane I cry with tenderness, and my crying does me good.

O my dear Marianna!

What a joy it will be to see that good old man again, and all my nearest and dearest! What tears! What consolation!

They won't let me tire myself, so I shan't write a long letter – and anyway, I wouldn't have the strength. If you only saw how wasted away your poor Maria is!

They tell me to keep calm, but they can't prevent my mind from racing away, and thinking of all those things make me cry with joy ... of the day when I'll go down to the parlour and see you all ... and my poor heart is filled with gladness.

But then you'll go away and leave me again – here, alone!

Praise be to God! At last I've seen my papa! You know how much I had to beg the doctor and the abbess to grant me this favour. Yesterday the doctor finally allowed me to leave the sick-room.

The weather was fine, and I could feel my poor, very unhealthy chest swell to breathe in the invigorating, morning air. Filomena lent me her arm to cross the garden. The sun was shining brightly and there were flowers ... I'd been so cold in those dismal big rooms that were practically dark! The leaves barely rustled because the breeze can't get into this enclosure, with such high walls all around. The gravel on the paths crunched under our feet, and two or three butterflies flitted from flower to flower ... It didn't amount to a great deal, admittedly, but you don't know how much this very little means to a poor recluse! Up above, at one of the dormitory windows, a canary sang sweetly ... it's true that it was in a cage, poor thing, and that had we been able to understand it we might have realized that it was grieving ... Yet all these insignificant things that cannot be put into words, that for most people pass unnoticed, constitute a wealth of joys for anyone who has nothing but the memory of fields, woods, life ... and they gladden the heart, if not the mind.

If you closed your eyes in that walled enclosure, you might forget that you were in the convent and imagine yourself to be surrounded by cheerful countryside, full of light and fresh air ... and to be free. Then the sight of such high walls and windows all covered with grilles sends an involuntary shudder through your heart.

You see what I'm like! To think that this corner of land, a patch of sky, a vase of flowers could have sufficed to give me all the happiness on earth, if I hadn't experienced freedom and felt in my heart the gnawing fever of all the joys that lie outside these walls. And to think that if I fall ill again, if they put me back in that sick-room, I'll be deprived even of this garden, these little flowers, and this sun that doesn't come to visit the poor nuns who are ill because even its rays would be saddened . . .

O Marianna! What a thrill it gave me to see my beloved papa waiting for me in the parlour! And to put my trembling hands to the grille! I couldn't tell you whether it was a thrill of pleasure or pain. The good old man couldn't hold back his tears, to see how pale and wasted I am. Gigi cried as well, and so did Giuditta, and I with my weak heart, who am so feeble and give way to tears over nothing, burst into sobs that brought relief to me. I wanted to throw myself into his arms, but there was that hard, cold grille between us, between father and daughter who were seeing each other after being on the point of never doing so again . . . I'd never fully understood until then, all that's hateful about life in an enclosed order.

When we had given vent to our tears, my father questioned me in great detail about my illness. He tried to smile, and comfort me, and every so often sobs would choke his voice, while tears fell on his grey beard and he didn't notice . . . It broke my heart! Yet it was supposed to be a joyful occasion, wasn't it? Giuditta was there, looking so pale! She was also crying. I gazed at her closely, as though I could see in her something new, and indefinable. I wanted to sob or cry out aloud in her arms, and her affection made my heart ache. I gazed at her and my eyes filled with tears, and through my tears I could see another very pale face, beside hers, that temptation conjured up before me . . .

O Marianna! This weakness come from my long illness. These hallucinations are the work of the devil. O God, help me!

And in those moments that should have been sacred, coming between me and those dearest to me was the nun who accompanied me, an outsider indifferent to this joy, this sorrow, these tears . . . Don't you think even tears have their own modesty? There was also my stepmother who wouldn't allow us the blessed relief of tears, on the grounds that crying was bad for me. Among all these cold, hard, unforgiving things, the iron grating was the least hostile.

How quickly those two hours that I was allowed to stay in the parlour flashed past! Eventually all those people that I cherish, who are a part of me, had to leave. My eyes followed them to the door, but when they were about to cross the threshold my heart failed me, I felt as though I were going out my mind. I called out loud to my father, almost beside myself, as if I were never going to see him again. I wanted an excuse to keep him for a few minutes longer, but I didn't know what to say, and I burst into tears. We all cried and no one could find a single word to say. My papa promised to return the next day. Then he really did leave, and I felt the sound of the door closing reverberate in my heart. I gripped the iron grille convulsively, and kept my eyes fixed on that closed door . . . My God, those were the worst moments! The nuns helped me back to my cell, and only when I was alone, with no one to see me, could I go down on my knees and give way to sobs.

Now I'm calmer. I've thank the Lord for allowing me to see my papa again. I've asked His forgiveness for this grief, which is an offence, because I'd already accepted this life of privation and sorrow, I'd vowed to dedicate myself entirely to Him . . . and the world still binds me with its most tenacious ties.

Merciful God, am I to blame if I haven't the strength to break these ties?

My dear Marianna, won't you come to visit this poor invalid one of these days? Come, please, do. I so badly need to see you!

I wonder what you'll think of me – a nun who moans and complains, and writes to you in secret? When I stoop to examining myself, I find myself so culpable, so abject, that I don't understand how you can still favour me with your friendship . . . My sin is monstrous, admittedly; yet I feel there's something more culpable than I am for my misfortune . . . and for this reason, God will forgive me. There are times when, if I didn't write to you, all the pain inside me would scream out of every pore . . .

Do you know, Marianna, the same temptation still possesses me? I have the same serpent still lurking here, in my heart! When I talk to you about anything else and try to hide it from you, from myself, then it bites me even more sharply, piercing me with its poisonous fangs. I'm afraid of being damned. I struggle against the Devil and he tightens his grip on me . . . I'm in his possession, do you understand? He possesses me! Now that I'm weakened by my illness, I haven't the strength to fight any more. I don't want to die, because I'm afraid of hell . . . because I love my sin!

Forgive me, my dearest sister! Even I'm appalled by what I write, by what I think . . . I can't pray to God any more because I daren't raise my eyes to Him . . .

My God, what have I done? What ever have I done?

I still love him! More than ever! Insanely! And I'm a nun, and he's married – to my sister! It's horrible, monstrous! I'm damned to perdition! But what fault is it of mine? How can I have earned such harsh punishment? Now that I'm buried alive, this love has grown into a fury, a raging frenzy! I no longer recall those moments of bliss, I no longer feel those timorous joys . . . Here, in my mind, in my heart, before my eyes, there's always a fearsome figure that makes me burn with anguish and passion . . . I hear a voice calling me from the world of the living . . . Listen . . . Maria! Maria! The name I had when I was alive

... Now Maria is dead ... and quaking all over, in a cold sweat from the terror in her limbs, because she feels the hand of the devil dragging her by the hair into the abyss ...

Seeing all these virgins, so pure and innocent, as they kneel and pray, and feeling that I'm the only guilty one among them, having to hide my remorse, when it increasingly torments me, and with the most comforting religious practices turned into yet another sin for a poor fallen woman! And being forced to deceive God ... Oh!

Every Sunday I go and kneel in the confessional-box, but alas, I haven't the strength to admit to this terrible transgression ... I even invent sins I haven't committed, as though to compensate for what I never dare say, what I jealously hide in my heart, as a she-wolf hides her young in a cave.

I think I must be mad, Marianna ... I'd like to tear my hair out, and rip open my chest with my fingernails. I'd like to howl like a wild beast, and shake these grilles that imprison my body, torture my spirit, and provoke my nervousness ...

What if I really were to go mad? I'm scared ... so scared ... A shudder runs through every fibre of my being, and the blood turns to ice in my veins.

I'm scared of that poor Sister Agata who's been locked up in the lunatics' cell for fifteen years. Do you remember that ghastly, thin, pale face, those wild, dull-witted eyes, those bony hands with long fingernails, those bare arms and that white hair? She's never stops prowling round, in the confined space of her tiny room. She clutches the iron bars and appears at the grille like some wild beast, half-naked, howling and snarling! And do you remember, there's a frightful convent tradition by which that cell is never left empty, and when one poor lunatic dies there's always some other miserable wretch to be locked inside? Marianna, I'm scared that I'm to succeed Sister Agata when God takes pity on her and calls her to Him.

I'm feverish. I shall die young. O God, don't punish me

so harshly! I'm scared, I'm scared of that white hair, those eyes, that pallor, that grimace, those hands that clutch at the bars of the grille ... What if I were to become like that! Oh, no! no!

It's night, and all is silence. The window's open. I heard a shopkeeper arguing with his wife, and in the end he beat her! Lucky, lucky woman! Then came the footsteps of someone out late: someone with a home, a family, and cherished possessions ... Why do I think of these things that make me cry? Why am I sickly and weak-minded? Why am I at fault? Oh, I'd forgotten about my fault!

Now, let me tell you how terrible my transgression is: how it recurs in every guise. On Sunday I was in the chancel, attending mass. I felt such peace, calmness and serenity in my heart. It seemed to me that at last God had taken pity on me and forgiven me. I prayed, with my eyes fixed on a man standing below, in the church, leaning against a pillar. He was of the same build, with the same black hair and a certain similarity of bearing. I'd have sacrificed what little hope of life was left to me, if he had only looked up at the chancel. I watched, and at times I thought it was definitely him ... and then the blood would start rushing round my head. When mass was over, he turned to go, and I prayed to the Virgin that he would look up at her statue, which is by the chancel, so that I could see his face, but he left, and I couldn't be sure it was him. I remained there, for I don't know how long, as if turned to stone, staring at the pillar that a man who might have been a complete stranger had been leaning against.

I want to see him! I want to see him! Just once! Just for one moment! O God, would it be such a great sin to see him? Only to see him ... from afar ... through the grille! He won't see me. He won't know that behind the grille there's a woman here dying, damned to everlasting punishment for his sake ...

Why did they take him away from me? Why did they steal my Nino from me? My heart, my love, my share of paradise ... Murderers, who killed my body, and are still torturing my soul!

Oh, how I love him! How I love him! I'm a nun ... I know! Who cares! I love him! He's my sister's husband, and I love him! It's a sin, a monstrous crime ... I love him, I love him!

I want to see him! I want to see him! If only for the last time! I'll wait for him at the window of the bell-tower overlooking the street. I'll wait there every day ... he's bound to pass by ... once, just once ... God will send him this way ...

God – O Marianna, how that word terrifies me! I'm raving, you can tell ... I'm beside myself ... I don't know what's wrong with me ... it must be fever ... or nerves ... I must be mad ...

I saw him, Marianna! I saw him! I suffered this additional agony! Praise be to God!

He went by with some of his friends, but he didn't even look up. Perhaps he didn't remember that his poor Maria from Monte Ilice was in this convent . . . a pale, dying Maria, who cries, and shivers with fever, and keeps him always in her heart . . . The sparkle in my eyes didn't dazzle him! He talked and laughed, with a cigar in his mouth, and the smoke rose to my window . . . I saw him, yes, yes, him, his face, clothes, movements, and I was scared of that smiling man, smoking and talking to his friends . . . Isn't that horrible, and monstrous?

Then he disappeared. He turned the corner into another street and I lost sight of him.

All those people continued to stroll and chat and enjoy themselves, and didn't notice that he wasn't there any more. Where was he? Where did he go? Home? To my sister . . . to his wife!

If only I were a tiger, or a demon! I'd tear my flesh to pieces, poison the air with my desperation, blot out the sun with my sorrow.

Damn! Damn me, him, everybody!

O God, God, what do you want of me?

Marianna, I ask your forgiveness, and the forgiveness of everyone I might have scandalized with my sins, just as I've asked forgiveness of merciful God . . . What must you have thought of me – of this abject sinner who spends her life weeping and praying at the foot of the Cross in order to purge her transgressions?

We had a special series of spiritual exercises. A very renowned preacher was called in, and speaking through him, God's voice thundered in the semi-darkness of the church with its black-curtained windows. How dreadful the word of the Lord is! No, it was my sins, my guilty conscience, and my remorse that made it frightening. For my heart tells me that the word of God cannot but resonate with infinite love and mercy.

How upset I was by those sermons! They instilled me with fear and terror. God seemed cruel. I saw the blast of His divine anger strike from above the altar, I heard a snarling of demons that was lost in the dome, and I saw the black wings of bats etched against the shadows of the vaulting. God spoke of hell, and of the damned . . . and all night long I thought I heard the lamentations of the souls in torment, weeping and wailing in the next world . . . And I was filled with dread, of myself and my sin.

Now I feel completely deranged . . . my heart tries in vain to take refuge in the thought of divine mercy . . . My sin is monstrous. Can I ever be forgiven? The preacher wasn't clear about that – he listed every transgression, threatening divine retribution against all the most wicked sins, but he dared not even include mine among them. His mind must have shunned the enormity of it!

Good God, what's become of me? Perhaps I've even forfeited the right to invoke you! A depraved sinner, condemned to suffer your anger, can I still listen to your word? Can I still prostrate myself at your feet among these virgins that are your chosen?

Marianna, it's dreadful to be abandoned even by the Lord! Yet there are times when temptation tells me that I'm innocent, that I'm blameless of my sin, that God might forgive me ... Why am I lost? What have I done?

It's the devil that suggests these doubts to me, and it's the devil that possesses me!

I consider myself damned. I'm filled with fear and loathing of myself, with remorse and terror. Yet I still love my God, and I wish I could unburden my soul of its immense anguish at the foot of the crucifix. But I can't, I can't ... I'm damned!

The nights! If you only knew what the nights were like – when the light burns out, and the shadows waver, and the furniture creaks, and the silence is full of whisperings and indistinct sounds. They're nights of deep terror, of sepulchral mysteries, the snarling of demons, the howls of the damned, an unholy rustling of wings. Everything's so gloomy – that long, dark and silent corridor, the dead lying beneath our feet, that church, those lamps and pictures – grotesque figures appear on the walls, and above my bed, at the foot of the crucifix, there's a shapeless skull ... there's the fear of the air you breathe, of a silence that conceals sinister noises, of the space around you, of the weight of the blankets on your body ... I daren't cry out because I'm afraid of awakening terrible echoes, of feeling a thousand horrible shapes settling on my flesh. Sleep is troubled, fraught with nightmares. I often wake with a cry, bathed in a cold sweat and tears.

Why was that sermon so frightening? Why is the word of God so terrible?

O Lord, have mercy even on this wretched sinner, have mercy even on this lost soul!

Thank you, Lord, thank you! I feel reborn. I feel purified by your forgiveness. I cried and prayed so hard that my wretchedness aroused your compassion. Now I'm calm and resigned. I don't want to think any more, I don't want to be alone. Thinking is our downfall, our temptation. I shan't write to you again, Marianna, because writing to you means remembering, and I don't want to remember you, or my father, or anybody! Forgive me, my loved ones . . . The heart is a great danger: if we could rip out our hearts, we'd be nearer to God!

O, the Lord will give me strength . . .

If I were to die right now, I think the angels would smile on me . . . but, no, Marianna, even this desire is a sin: we must remain here in this world for as long as God wills. My soul, which is craven and weak, has so little desire to remain here that it sees with a wrongful sense of joy how rapidly my illness progresses from day to day.

My poor Marianna, you should see me now! I've become a skeleton. You should see my hands, face and eyes! My poor chest is entirely consumed with a burning fever. You should hear me cough. If only you could be with me when the pain of my illness exceeds my courage.

It's better that you don't see me again, Marianna, that no one should ever see me again! I have what I might call the shame of the sick. In his providential blindness, my papa always finds countless reasons for deluding himself and not noticing the state that I'm in.

O God, I belong to you, just as I am, with my failings and weaknesses, with my faults and my guilt, and with my immense love for you. Have pity on me, God, have pity on me! Let me not think! That's my only prayer, that I might live and die in acceptance of no other thought but of You.

O my God, why have you forsaken me?

There's no word for what I feel! To have such a sense of guilt, to be so fearful of your own sin, and unable to break away from it . . .

That sermon! Still, that terrible voice is in my ears! The horror of it! I see hell gaping before me. I feel lost, like Satan, in the abyss of God's abandonment . . . and I love Nino just the same! I'm afraid of demons, and I think of him! I dare to raise my supplicant eyes to the altar, and I think of him! My mind is full of spectres and flames and dreadful faces . . . and I smile and yearn for him – the embodiment of sin, temptation and the devil!

Let me tell you what happened, Marianna! I was on the terrace, sitting by that little chapel that we used to decorate with garlands of flowers. It was just after sunrise. You could hear the many sounds of the streets, and the birds singing. The sky was blue, and the sea sparkling bright, and a fragrant breeze filled my poor ailing lungs . . . And I mused and mused . . .

You see how the tempting devil called thought treacher-ously sneaks inside us through every pore and mercilessly penetrates our minds! I contemplated the little flower with its trembling dew-drops, the smoke rising from the chim-neys, the sails of a ship disappearing into the brightness of the sea, the singing that floated up from the street. Was I dreaming? I don't know. Two butterflies followed each other from flower to flower – one had wings of gold, the other's were all white. With a touch of mischievousness, the one with snow-white wings hid inside a pretty flower, even whiter than itself, and its poor companion searched for it, fluttering its little golden wings in distress. How timidly those butterflies approached the petals of that lovely bloom! Then the other one peered into the heart of the flower, and may have smiled, and then hid in there as well. What did they say to each other? What were they fighting over? What was going on inside their tiny minds? How much happiness was enclosed within that little flowerhead? A small bird cheeped on the ridge of the chapel roof, and beat its wings so rapidly that in the dawn sunlight its feathers looked as if they were made of golden straw. 'Come, come!' it said, and it seemed to be crying. Who can tell? Perhaps it really was crying. Who was it waiting for? Who was it calling? Then it took off, swift and straight and sure in its flight. Where was it hurrying? It was free, and away it flew! By a large crack in the wall, a lizard basked in the sun. You should have seen how happy that little creature was! How its little sides panted, and its tiny head moved, and its eyelets shone! Perhaps it was blessing that ray of sunshine, which it, too, was enjoying, and that dew-drop which the petal let fall. Who has ever considered all the joys around us? The happiness that exists in the worm that crawls on the ground, and within the invisible atom? Then came the sound of a carriage: the horses had harness-bells – you know how cheerful harness-bells sound, how reminiscent they are of the countryside, of green meadows and dusty roads, of flowering hedgerows and larks that dart in front of the horses ... Then the screech of a pulley could be heard, and the bright, fresh voice of a woman singing one of those nonsensical, popular songs that are deeply moving – it was a serving-girl, drawing water from a well. Why was she so happy? What was she thinking of? Her native village? Sunday mass? The small square in front the church, crowded with young people dressed in their best clothes? The familiar voice that used to come and sing that old song outside her door?

All these things spoke, and what they said was, 'Nino! Nino!' I looked round in search of him, and I saw him! I saw him at the window of a nearby house. It was him, it really was – with a pipe in his mouth and his elbows resting on the window-sill. He was taking in all the joyfulness of a beautiful morning. Oh, my poor heart! I seemed to remember once being told that my sister had moved to a house near the convent, but God had spared me from

thinking about it ... Now there he was before me ...
Why? O God, why? What was he doing? What was he
thinking? Could he see me? No, no! His eyes were distracted ... yet he should have been able to see me, in my
black habit and white veil, with my arms outstretched ...
What was in that man's heart? Oh, the tears I shed! O
Lord, let me see him on his own, and I shall be for ever
grateful! O my God, let me not see my sister, let me not
see her!

Nino! It's me, over here! Can't you see me? Don't you
remember? What's the matter? What have I done wrong?
Oh, my head! Nino! Look at me! See how pale I am! Hear
how laboured my breathing is! O Nino, please, look at
me!

He turned round. I saw a figure behind him ... a dress
... I fled because I was losing my mind! God, what agony!
I went and retired to my cell, like some wounded beast
going to earth ... Oh, what burning pain! My head! My
poor head!

It was such a dreadful day, with that figure continually
before me, and my heart pierced with anguish the whole
time.

I'm almost insane. I feel something clutching my flesh
and dragging me back up to the terrace ... to see that
man, the mere thought of whom breaks my heart ... I
wish I could spend all my days there, and die of sorrow
with my eyes fixed on that window. I tried to think of
God, and God seemed cruel. I tried to think of that
sermon, and it seemed to me unjust. All the furies of hell
are tormenting my heart ... Listen, Marianna, listen to this
lost soul – because I want to be lost, I want to be damned!
At night when everyone was asleep, I went up on to the
terrace, in bare feet, squeezing my chest so that the nuns
wouldn't hear the beating of my scared and cowardly
heart, and stealing through the shadows like a ghost. It
took me half an hour to get there – half an hour of terror,
and anxiety, and inward strife, taking fright at the slightest
sound, holding my breath at every door, collapsing in

exhaustion on every stair ... If he could have seen me! Then when I got up there, and I saw the stars above my head, and that lighted window, not even I could tell you what happened inside me ... Listen! I'll tell you what I saw, and you'll suffer as I did ... I wish for all those I love to suffer ... Eleven o'clock was striking. The chimes had a sharpness of vibration that stabbed like a knife. The streets were still crowded ... there were people strolling and laughing – you could even hear what those that were closest were saying. You could see that lighted window in the darkness, staring at me with its wide-open eye. I had often spent the evening lost in reverie, gazing at some distant light shining in some far-off room, trying to imagine all the care and affection, all the little troubles that to my poor mind seem another joy of family life, and the conversation, and the talk probably going on round that solitary light. But this window had a fiery reflection. I couldn't look at it without feeling a heat rushing through all my veins. It was him! It was him! It was his house, occupying his life and his affections, in all peaceful serenity, with all the blessings of the family. The room was wall-papered in a pattern of big, blue flowers; by the window was an armchair, and further back, on a little table, were numerous objects that I couldn't distinguish, but some of which gleamed in the candlelight. Imagine the tabernacle – I can think of no other way to describe it ... Each of those objects had the imprint of his hand on it, and he had sat in that armchair a hundred times. Why was the room empty? It seemed to be afraid, and it also frightened me ... Then a door opened and a woman came in. My sister! How beautiful she looked! She was able to touch every one of those objects and to sit in that chair. She came to the window, blocking out the light – cruel, cruel woman! – and she leaned on the window-sill. She seemed to be looking at me. I was scared of that face turned towards me that remained in shadow. I hid behind the chapel. How I trembled! How my heart pounded! After a while she suddenly drew back and went to open the door by which she'd entered. It was him! He took her hand and kissed it. God! O God, let me die! Even if I'm damned!

You can have no idea what frenzy, what furious delight there is in inflicting atrocious torture on yourself ... punishing yourself because you can't punish others. I watched that man kiss that woman ... the man, Nino, and she, my sister! I watched them sitting together, talking and holding hands, exchanging smiles and taking turns to steal kisses from each other. I knew all the sweet things they were saying to each other, and by a miracle of intuition I saw the smallest movement of his face, and the expression in his eyes. No one could have seen what I saw. My dry eyes opened wide; my heart stopped beating; and there was a whiff of the devil inside me ... And this spectacle lasted nearly an hour! An hour out there, with bare feet, burning with fever, shuddering with horror, filling my lungs with anguish and fury. In order to see him, I inflicted that terrible joy on myself, a joy with the fiery edge of anguish ... and I returned there every evening, despite the risk, the fever and delirium ... I saw him! What does it matter how? I saw him! I spent days out on the terrace, with a blazing sun beating down on my bare head, my mind dazed, befuddled, and dizzy, my eyes smarting, and my body on fire with fever, for nothing more than to see him, just for a moment, passing from one room to another!

Ah, if sorrow could kill!

God, let me die! Let me die!

For pity's sake! Have mercy! I can't take any more.

I'm ill, Marianna. The fever's in my brain, and my head's burning. From my little cell I can hear the screams of poor Sister Agata. I feel like screaming, too, and scratching the plaster off the walls with my fingernails, as she does.

Why have they shut me up in here? What have I done? Why these grilles, veils, and bolts? Why these lugubrious prayers, dim lights, and pale, frightening faces? Why this darkness and silence? What have I done? My God, what have I done?

I want to leave, I want to get out of here! I don't want to stay any more! I want to escape . . . Help me, Marianna, help me! I'm scared. I'm frantic. I want light. I want to run free!

Marianna, why are you abandoning me as well? Tell my father to come and fetch me out of this tomb. Tell him that I'm dying, that I'm being murdered. Tell him I shall smash my head against these walls. Tell him I'll be good, that I'll love everybody; I'll be the servant of the house, I'll be content with a kennel, as long as I get out of here. Tell him I haven't done anything wrong. Why is he, too, being so ruthless? Will no one take pity on me? Will no one help? Will it not occur to any of the passers-by in the street, with the grace of happiness in their hearts, that there might be some miserable wretch locked up inside here, dying in despair? Shout! Yell with me! Cry for help! Tell all who can hear you that I'm kept in here by force, that I've done no wrong. I'm innocent . . . Tell them this is a place of death . . . there's a smell of dead bodies here . . . and you can hear the screams of a madwoman . . .

The madwoman wants to escape, too, poor thing! They keep her locked up behind iron bars ... She can't sleep, she can't die ... She prowls that small space allowed to her, from morning to night, raging and howling ... the poor wretch! It's frightful!

What if they were to lock me up with Sister Agata? How ghastly! How horrible! What if I were to go mad?

O Marianna, I wish I could jump out of the highest window, but they're all barred!

What torture! What agony! Even death, suicide and hell are denied to me! What have I done? What ever have I done? I swear, I'm innocent!

Listen, I shan't love him any more! I'll pluck him out of my heart ... I'll rock his children's cradle ... I'll go far away ... Let them do what they will with me – anything – as long as they take me away from here.

Tell them I didn't know what they wanted of me when they made me a nun, that I didn't know I'd have to be imprisoned for ever, that I was mad, that I'll lose my soul here, that I haven't long to live, not long at all ... So why don't they let die in peace?

Yesterday the doctor came to see me. Why did they send for him? He kept looking at me in a strange way ... He took my pulse. I'm all right, I feel nothing at all ... He asked me lots of questions I didn't understand. What does this mean? What do they want of me? They're watching me. They're keeping me at a distance ... What's happened? Are they trying to frighten me?

I told the doctor that I want to get out of here. I promised to be good, to work and do whatever was wanted of me, as long as they let me out. The kindly old man smiled and was unnervingly quick to promise me everything I asked of him.

What does this mean, Marianna, what does this mean? I'm alone. I look at myself, and I think I'm dreaming. I don't know what's happened, but it must be something dreadful ... something really horrible!

It's because I'm frightened by Sister Agata's screams that are audible even from here, whenever the poor creature has one of her fits.

Today I spent the whole day staring at the door by which I came into this place ... a solid black door with huge bolts, that only opens to let in victims, that you can never return through ...

And I came in by that door! I was free outside, and I crossed that threshold on my own two feet! No one dragged me across, no one pushed me! My God, how did it happen? Was I mad? I must have been in a trance. What on earth lies on the other side of that door? What goes through the mind of any passer-by? How bright the sky must be! Nino's on the other side! Isn't he?

They wouldn't let me stay there looking at it any longer. Why not? Is that wrong as well? They took me away. I do whatever they want ... I'm meek ... I'm scared ... I'm scared they'll lock me up with the mad-woman ...

Nino! Nino! Where's Nino? I want to see him! Why won't they let me see him? He's the only one I want to see. I don't want to see my father, my brother, or my sister . . .

My sister! She stole him from me! Why did she steal him? Didn't she know he was mine? Why can't I see him? Tell him to come . . . Tell him to come and free me. We'll go to Monte Ilice together . . . we'll go and hide in the chestnut grove . . . alone . . . like the creatures of the wild. Tell him to come, to come armed with his gun . . . that way, he'll frighten my goalers . . . they're women . . . they'll be scared . . . he'll kill them if necessary . . . he'll save me . . . he'll find me here in my cell . . . and I'll throw my arms round his neck! Yes, the nun!

The nun will escape . . . she'll run away with him . . . with her sister's husband . . . she'll steal him back . . . They'll go far away . . . they'll walk and walk . . . they'll go to the mountains, to the woods . . . they'll be together and they won't be afraid . . . they won't hear Sister Agata screaming . . . There'll be the stars, and the rain, and the sound of thunder, and he'll knock on the window . . . She'll cough . . . He'll say, 'Maria! Maria!'

Who's Maria? I think I knew her . . . Maria's dead, she's run away . . . Where is she?

Oh, my poor head! Listen, Marianna . . . it's night-time now . . . everyone's asleep . . . no one will see me . . . I'll creep downstairs . . . across the garden . . . it's dark . . . the gravel on the paths won't make any noise out of compassion for me . . . I'll go up to the door . . . that nasty door will say no! And I'll cry, and beg, and go down on my knees . . . I'll say that Nino's waiting for me, that I have to go to him . . . and not being a nun, the door will then take pity on me . . . and let me slip through the keyhole . . . then I'll be outside . . . where there are sunshine and fresh air, streets, and people, and him! Where you can shout, and run, and cry, and hug the people you love . . . I'll run away, I'll run away ... because Sister Agata clings to me if she sees me ... and I'll go and knock at his door and say, 'Here I am!' And he'll hold out his arms to me ... No, that's wicked, that's a sin! I'll say to Giuditta, 'I'm your sister ... your poor sister who's suffered so much ... they wanted to kill your poor sister, they wanted to bury her alive ... they wanted to lock her up with Sister Agata ... let me stay here, I'll be your servant, I shan't love him any more ... I'll just look at him, through the keyhole, when you're asleep and don't need to look at him.' O God! I'm so happy, Marianna, I'm so happy! Thank you, God, thank you!

Help, Marianna, help! My father, help! Nino! Nino! Kill them! Kill them! Gigi! Giuditta! Help! They're laying hands on me, they're dragging me by the hair! Help! They're hitting me! Ouch, ouch, my hair ... my arms ... they're all bruised! There's blood! They say I'm mad! Mad! Ah, Sister Agata! Sister Agata!

What do they want? What do these people want? Why are they laying hands on me? I'm innocent ... I haven't done anything wrong ... I want to get away from here, I want to escape ... there are corpses ... and demons ... I'm scared! God has abandoned me! Don't abandon me as well! Nino! Nino! You're brave – help me!

I've no strength left in me ... they're dragging me off ... they're dragging me off ... Where to? Where to? My God!

Ah! The lunatics' cell! Sister Agata's cell! No! No! For pity's sake, I'm not mad! I'm scared! I shan't do it again ... Here I am ... I'll stay here, I'll be good, I'll pray ... What do you want? What do you want? Send for my father, send for Marianna ... they'll tell you I'm not mad! Ah, Nino! Nino! Why can't you hear me? Nino? Such yells and screams and tears! Such foaming at the mouth and bleeding! Nino! Help! Here! Help! I'll bite, I'm a wild animal! No! Please! No! Not in there! Nino!

Dear Signora Marianna,

I was asked by poor Sister Maria – God rest her soul! – to see that you received the little silver crucifix and handwritten pages that I sending you via our gate-keeper.

I hesitated for a long time before reaching a decision in such a delicate matter of conscience. The deceased's last wishes were certainly sacred to me, but our rule forbids us from disposing of anything whatsoever, even in the case of death, without the permission of Mother Superior. I hope that I've been enlightened by the grace of the Holy Spirit, for this is what seemed to me the best solution, to the greater benefit of God and a fellow- human being.

I resorted to an equivocation to obtain this permission, which might have been difficult to obtain otherwise. I told Mother Superior of Sister Maria's last wish, and I showed her the crucifix that the poor young girl had bequeathed on her death-bed, together with the handwritten pages, as if these were of no significance and served only as a wrapping for the small gift.

I don't know what these pages contain. However, had they been read, I doubt that permission would ever have been granted to send them to any outsider. On the other hand, if they'd ever been found inside the convent, I fear they might have given rise to scandal, very detrimental to the memory of the departed and of great harm to her soul.

Under the impression that it was a matter of little significance, Mother Superior readily granted permission, without feeling obliged to seek the chaplain's advice, and I have the satisfaction today of fulfilling my duty without incurring any blame. You, my dear lady, will receive the small package in the same state it was left in by the dear departed. There are nine pages in all, four of blue paper, two sheets of writing paper, and the last three written on the envelopes of other letters, all carefully numbered. The package is tied with a black ribbon and contains:

1. A small silver crucifix
2. A lock of hair.
3. Some rose petals.

If my poor friend had not in her dying moments shown such attachment to these two or three dried petals, I would not have taken the liberty of sending them as well, in the fear it might have seemed to you an unseemly jest on my part. But the dying girl tried to kiss them when the pains that consumed her became more agonizing, and she expired with these dead petals on her lips.

May God ease her suffering in purgatory for what the poor martyr has suffered here on earth! She died like a saint, God bless her!

On that fateful day when she was mistakenly thought to be mad, her ruined health was dealt a final blow. Jesus and Mary! What a day that was! How the poor girl suffered! She was so frail, so weak, she could hardly stand, and yet it took more than four lay sisters to drag her to the lunatics' cell! I think I can still hear those desperate, totally inhuman screams ringing in my ears, and still see her face, crazed with terror, and bathed in tears that would break your heart . . . She was unconscious when they opened the cell. They left her there, on the bare floor . . .God forgive me! I think that poor mad Sister Agata was the only one to show the poor girl any pity, because she did not venture to do her any harm. She gazed at her with those dull eyes, and lay on the floor beside her, touching and shaking her as though trying to revive her. When the doctor came, he found her still in that state. He then gave orders for her to be taken to the sick-room. When Mother Superior, in the interests of the community, expressed fears that Sister Maria might have another fit, the doctor reassured her, saying that it would only be for a little while . . . And indeed she did not long survive . . .

The poor sick girl regained consciousness in the infirmary. You can't imagine how heart-breaking it was just to see the terrfied look that she gave us . . . for she couldn't move, poor soul! She had no strength left in her. She

lingered on like this for three days – three days of agony.
She couldn't move or speak any more. She lay there, just
as they'd placed her, with her eyes wide open, trembling
the whole time, with a breathless wheeze in her throat.
Not until dawn of the third day did she manage to convey
to me with her eyes that she wanted her head turned
towards the window, and when she saw the sky her eyes
filled with tears.

Poor Sister Maria! She was no more than a skeleton.
Only her eyes – those beautiful eyes! – were still alive. She
told me so many things with her eyes, and the last dregs of
her wretched life were fraught with pain. When I raised
her head, she looked at me in such a way that I could not
hold back the tears. She tried to lift her arm to throw it
round my neck, but she hadn't the strength, and sighed. So
I took her hand and she squeezed it – she squeezed it as
though she were speaking to me.

At about ten o'clock they administered the last rites to
her. She took communion with such serenity and faith that
it seemed that all the saints and angels in heaven were
gathered round her bed. God bless her! She remained like
that all day, while litanies were recited round her. When
the sun went down she seemed distressed again. She wept
so freely that one of the lay sisters was moved to pity and
wiped the poor girl's face – it was bathed with tears, and
she couldn't see us any more. Then she moved her lips as
though to call. I bent down over her. She strained to put
her face close to mine, and whispered in my ear this last
wish, breathing with such difficulty it was heart-breaking
. . . Her wheeze was suffocating her. I guessed rather than
heard what she said. I ran to fetch the package that she
wanted, and seeing it in my hands, she gave an angelic
smile . . . When her wheeze wasn't suffocating her, she
kept saying, 'For him! For him!' She must have been
delirious. She wanted me to show her everything: the
pages, the hair, the crucifix, the dry petals. She kissed
them, she kissed them so much that I removed one of those
petals from her lips after she had died.

Then she turned her head away with a gentle sigh. She seemed to have fallen asleep ... and it was an everlasting sleep.

Poor Sister Maria!

Yet now she's among the blessed, praying to the Lord for us wretched sinners that in our weakness mourn her death. I must add, to the credit of Mother Superior and the whole community, and to the comfort of all those who loved her in her lifetime, that her funeral was extremely moving. More than thirty masses were celebrated at every altar in the church, and there were more than a hundred candles burning at the De Profundis. Please remember me in your prayers.

> I remain, respectfully, your most devoted servant,
>
> Sister Filomena

CHRONOLOGY

1840 2 September. Giovanni Verga was born in Catania, Sicily. His family were landowners and members of the minor nobility.

1848/9 Year of Revolutions in Italy.

1857 Wrote his first novel, "Amore e Patria" (unpublished).

1858 Enrols as a student of law at Catania University.

1859 Beginning of the Italian War of Independence.

1860 Insurrections in Sicily in April are followed by the arrival of Garibaldi and his volunteers who take Sicily from the Bourbons.
Verga joins the National Guard founded after the arrival of Garibaldi. He is one of the founders and the editor of the weekly political magazine Roma degli Italiani.

1861 The Bourbons are forced out of Naples, and Garibaldi surrenders Naples and Sicily to Victor Emanuel, the Piedmontese king. In plebiscites the people of Southern Italy vote to be part of the newly formed Italian Kingdom under Victor Emanuel.
Verge abandons his legal studies and publishes his first novel, "I Carbonari della Montagna," at his own expense.

1863 His patriotic novel, "Sulle lagune", is published in a magazine.
His father dies.

1864	Florence becomes the new capital of Italy, replacing Turin.
1865	Verga's first visit to Florence. He becomes a frequent visitor and takes up permanent residence in 1869.
1866	20 July, naval battle at Lissa. The Austrians retreat from Venice which becomes part of Italy. His novel, "Una Peccatrice" is published.
1869	Settles in Florence, where he meets Luigi Capuana, the realist writer and theorist. Begins an affair with the 18-year-old Giselda Foljanesi.
1870	Rome is taken, and becomes the Italian capital in 1871.
1871	Zola's "La Fortune de Rougon", the first book in the Rougon–Macquart cycle, is published. Zola's theories and Naturalism become increasingly important and controversial in Italy. Verga publishes "Storia di una capinera", which is an immediate success.
1872	Goes to live in Milan, where he spends most of the next 20 years. Frequents the literary salons of the city, making a name for himself in the capital of Italian publishing. Giselda Foljanesi marries the Catanese poet Mario Rapisardi.
1873	"Eva" is published, and is criticized for its immorality.
1874/6	"Tigre Reale", "Eros", and the novella "Nedda" are published.

1877   "L'Assommoir" of Zola is published and has an overwhelming influence in Italy. Verga publishes his collected short stories, "Primavera e altri racconti."

1878   His mother dies, to whom he was greatly attached.

1880   "Vita dei Campi" is published. Visits Giselda Foljanesi.

1881   "I Malavoglia" is published. Verga is disappointed by its lack of success. Begins an affair with countess Dina Castellazi, who is married and in her twenties. It lasts most of his life.

1883   Goes to Paris, and visits Zola at Médan. Also goes to London. Publishes "Novelle Rusticane" and the novel "Il Marito di Elena", and "Per le Vie". Visits Catania where he sees Giselda Foljanesi. In December Rapisardi discovers a compromising letter from Verga to his wife, and so Giselda is forced to leave and settle in Florence.

1884   The play of "Cavalleria Rusticana" is put on with great success in Turin, with Eleonora Dusa playing Santuzza.
The end of Verga's affair with Giselda Foljanesi.

1886–7   Passes most of his time at Rome. The publication of a French translation of "I Malavoglia" is without success.

1888   Returns to live in Sicily.

1889   "Mastro-don Gesualdo" is published and is an immediate success. D'Annunzio publishes his novel, "Il Piacere".

1890   Mascagni's one act opera of "Cavalleria Rusticana" is put on and enjoys an overwhelming success. Verga sues Mascagni and Sonzogno for his share of the royalties.
First English translation of "I Malavoglia".

1891   Publishes a volume of stories, "I Ricordi del capitano d'Arce". Wins his case in the Court of Appeal, getting 143,000 lire (which was a large sum then and put an end to the financial problems which had beset him).

1895   Goes with Capuana to visit Zola in Rome.

1896   The defeat at Adua puts an end to Italy's colonial expansion. Verga criticizes the demonstrations against the war. Begins writing the third novel in his "I Vinti" cycle, "La Duchessa di Leyra", but never completes it.

1898   There are riots in Milan, after the price of bread is increased, which are violently put down by the army. Verga applauds their actions as a defence of society and its institutions.

1900–3   Various of his plays are put on, but Verga's energies turn away from his writing to managing his business interests and living quietly in Sicily.

1915   Declares himself in favour of Italian involvement in WW1, and anti-pacificism.

1920	His eightieth birthday is celebrated in Rome and Catania. In November he becomes a senator.
1922	27 January Verga dies in Catania. Mussolini comes to power.
1925/8	D. H. Lawrence translates "Mastro-don Gesualdo", "Vita dei Campi" and "Novelle Rusticane" into English.
1947	Luchino Visconti's film of "I Malavoglia" called "La Terra Trema".
1950	Eric Mosbacher's translation of "I Malavoglia".
1964	Raymond Rosenthal's American translation of "I Malavoglia".
1984	Dedalus publishes the D. H. Lawrence translations of "Mastro Don Gesualdo" and "Novelle Rusticane" (Short Sicilian Novels)
1985	Judith Landry's translation of "I Malavoglia".
1987	Dedalus publishes the D. H. Lawrence translation of "Vita dei Campi" under the title of "Cavalleria Rusticana".
1991	New Dedalus edition of "I Malavoglia".
1994	First English translation of "La Storia di una Capinera" by Christine Donougher published as "Sparrow (the Story of a Songbird)". Franco Zeffirelli's film of "La Storia di una Capinera" called "Sparrow".

HULL LIBRARIES

5 4072 0226 5403 6

DEVON & CORNWALL

ROUGH GUIDE STAYCATIONS

FROM STOCK

Kingston up

CW005948496

ROUGH
GUIDES

YOUR TAILOR-MADE TRIP ✦ STARTS HERE

Tailor-made trips and unique adventures crafted by local experts

Rough Guides has been inspiring travellers with lively and thought-provoking guidebooks for more than 35 years. Now we're linking you up with selected local experts to craft your dream trip. They will put together your perfect itinerary and book it at local rates.

Don't follow the crowd – find your own path.

HOW ROUGHGUIDES.COM/TRIPS WORKS

STEP 1

Pick your dream destination, tell us what you want and submit an enquiry.

STEP 2

Fill in a short form to tell your local expert about your dream trip and preferences.

STEP 3

Our local expert will craft your tailor-made itinerary. You'll be able to tweak and refine it until you're completely satisfied.

STEP 4

Book online with ease, pack your bags and enjoy the trip! Our local expert will be on hand 24/7 while you're on the road.